PLAYING FOR PRIDE

Timothy Tocher

PLAYING FOR PRIDE

Timothy Tocher

Meadowbrook Press

Distributed by Simon and Schuster
New York

Library of Congress Cataloging-in-Publication Data

Tocher, Timothy.
Playing for pride / by Timothy Tocher.
p.cm
Summary: When Laurie, a basketball hotshot, reluctantly tries out for the middle school softball team, she is surprised to find that she enjoys the game but afraid that everyone will expect too much of her.
Publisher's ISBN 978-0-88166-424-9
Simon and Schuster ISBN 978-0-689-02453-5
[1. Softball--Fiction. 2. Sportsmanship--Fiction. 3. Self-confidence--Fiction. 4. All-American Girls Professional Baseball League--Fiction. 5. New York (State)--Fiction.] I. Title.
PZ7.T5637 Pl 2002
[Fic]--dc21

Editorial Director: Christine Zuchora-Walske
Editors: Megan McGinnis and Angela Wiechmann
Production Manager: Paul Woods
Production Assistant: Peggy Bates
Cover Illustrator: Carol Heyer

Published by Meadowbrook Press
6110 Blue Circle Drive, Suite 237,
Minnetonka, Minnesota 55343

www.meadowbrookpress.com

BOOK TRADE DISTRIBUTION by Simon & Schuster, a division of Simon and Schuster, Inc., 1230 Avenue of the Americas, New York, New York 10020

16 15 14 13 12 12 11 10 9 8 7 6 5 4 3 2

Printed in the United States of America

Dedication

To Judy

Acknowledgments

Thanks to my mentor and publisher,
Bruce Lansky, for believing in Laurie and her teammates.
Thanks to my editors, Megan McGinnis,
for her invaluable assistance, and Angela Wiechmann,
for her keen eye and sense of story.

Contents

Chapter 1

Recruiting

"Yes! That's game," Laurie Bird Preston shouted as she watched her tenth—and winning—free throw fall through the net. She darted down the lane, scooped up the ball, and shot a lay-up.

A gust of wind, which was warm for late March in the Hudson Valley, blew her light brown hair across her face. Laurie tucked the hair behind her ears. "Want to play again?" she asked her two best friends, Li and Howard.

Li Tang shook her head, her shiny black ponytail swaying. "Nope," she said. "Three games are enough for me. How about you, Howard?"

Howard Goldstein pushed his glasses back into place on his nose. "No way. I'm done being beaten by you two."

"Besides," he added, "there's another game I'd like to play."

Laurie's eyes followed Howard's gaze to a worn baseball mitt lying on the edge of the court next to his ever-present laptop computer.

"Not again, Howard," she groaned. Ever since Laurie and Li's basketball team had won the New York state middle school championship a few weeks earlier, Howard had been trying to convince Laurie to go out for the softball team. She couldn't make him understand that just because the basketball season was over, she wasn't going to stop working on her game.

Laurie caught Howard gesturing to Li, and she knew she was about to be double-teamed.

"C'mon, Laurie." Li faced her friend. "Why shoot baskets by yourself when you could be playing softball with your friends?"

"The Cyclones are going to have a great team," Howard added, tucking his laptop under his arm and pounding his fist into his mitt. He was going to help manage the softball team just as he had the basketball team.

"But basketball is my game," Laurie countered. "If I'm going to be the best, I've got to practice year round."

"Softball might help," Howard coaxed. "You'll stay in better shape if you're working out with a team."

"And how can you pass up the excitement?" Li asked, her dark eyes shining. "What could beat competing against other schools, maybe even winning another championship?"

Laurie shrugged. Howard and Li were right. Working out with a team would keep her in good shape, and having another chance to win a championship would be exciting. Still, Laurie couldn't admit to her friends the real reason why she was reluctant to try out for softball: She was afraid she would embarrass herself.

Laurie had concentrated on basketball her whole life. She had played softball in gym class, but she'd never really been that good at it. Wouldn't everyone expect her to be a great player after seeing her play hoops? Why wreck her reputation by playing a sport she wasn't good at and might not even like?

"If you think Dawn and Jackie are good at basketball, you should see them play softball," Howard raved. "They both made All-League last year. No one can hit Dawn's fastball, and

Jackie's a great catcher. She can hit the ball a mile." Howard took a mock swing and barely managed to grab his falling laptop before it hit the ground.

"Maggie's going out, too," Li added, "and Jesse, and Wheezy, and Angela, and Eileen—"

Laurie laughed, "I get the picture!"

All her friends and former teammates were trying out for softball. Did she want to spend the spring by herself while her friends had fun as a team? Laurie was beginning to think she didn't.

"I know it's not the coach keeping you away," Li kidded.

Laurie's father had coached the Cyclones' basketball team and would run the softball squad as well.

"My dad has been great," Laurie admitted. "He wants me to play, but he hasn't put any pressure on me."

Li and Howard focused their eyes on her, grins fixed on their faces. Laurie felt herself weakening.

"Oh, okay," she sighed, tossing the basketball from hand to hand. "I'll give softball a try."

"All right!" Howard pumped his fist in the air.

"You're going to love it," Li promised. "Let's warm up a little. The first practice is tomorrow." She reached into her backpack, which lay on a nearby picnic table, and pulled out a softball and a mitt.

Laurie put a hand on her hip and cocked her head to the side. "You must have been pretty sure I'd say yes."

"Yeah, well, I knew you wouldn't want to miss any sports action," Li managed, giving Laurie a sheepish grin.

They left the basketball court to play a game called pickle on the park's open lawn. Howard tried to run between two bases while Li and Laurie threw the ball back and forth. When the girls succeeded in tagging Howard out three times, Li became the runner.

Between Li's speed and Howard's wild throws, Li's turn might have gone on forever. But the low growl of a big truck turning onto the street caused the three friends to quit the game.

A moving van crawled to a stop in front of the brown and white house next door to Laurie's grandmother's. The house had stood empty for as long as Laurie and her dad had lived with Grandma.

"Someone's moving in," Howard said. "I wonder if they have kids."

A small blue car pulled up behind the van. It had barely stopped when two girls shot from the back seat and ran across the overgrown lawn to the house. One was a preschooler, but the other, her long black hair streaming out from under a baseball cap, looked to be about eleven years old, the same age as Laurie and her friends.

A moment later a tall, athletic-looking man got out of the driver's side. A slight dark-haired woman stepped out of the passenger's side, then turned and reached into the back seat to bring out a baby in a car seat. The man draped his arm around the woman's shoulder, and they walked toward the house together.

"Do you think that girl is in our grade?" Laurie wondered.

Before Li or Howard could answer, they heard a familiar voice calling Laurie's name. Grandma Preston stood on the front steps, motioning for them to come to her. The three friends quickly gathered up their gear and ran across the street.

"It looks like our new neighbors are here," Grandma said, watching the movers as they began to unload the van.

"You knew they were coming and you didn't tell me?" Laurie asked, her eyes wide.

Grandma laughed. "It wasn't a secret, Laurie. I'd just heard that someone had rented the house, but I didn't know when they were moving in."

"What's their name? Where do they come from? How old are the kids?" Howard asked.

Grandma ruffled Howard's already messed-up hair. "I know their last name is Sanchez and they're from New York City. Take these muffins over and you can find out the rest." She handed Laurie a basket covered with a dishtowel.

Laurie, Howard, and Li raced to the new neighbors' house. They had reached the edge of the overgrown lawn when the girl in the baseball cap came out the front door, pounding a softball into the pocket of a mitt as she walked. When she saw the three friends approaching, she stopped and smiled shyly.

"Hi," Laurie and Li said together.

"Welcome to Compton," Howard added.

The girl stood a little taller. "I'm Carlotta."

"I'm Howard, and this is Laurie and Li. Laurie lives next door," Howard offered. "What grade are you in?"

"Fifth, and you?"

"We're in fifth grade, too," Li said. "Looks like you play softball. You're just in time to try out for the middle school team. First practice is tomorrow."

"I know. My dad called up the school last week." Carlotta waved her arms at the grass and trees. "It seems weird having all this green right outside my door."

Laurie wanted to know what it was like to live in such a huge city, but before she could ask Carlotta, a voice called out, "Carlotta, *por favor*."

"That's my mom," Carlotta explained. "I've got to take care of my sisters while the movers are working. I'll see you guys tomorrow."

"Oh, here," Laurie said, remembering the muffins. "My grandmother baked these for you."

"They smell great!" Carlotta grinned. "See you in school."

The next morning the guidance counselor brought Carlotta to Laurie and Howard's classroom. Carlotta shook hands with their teacher, Ms. Brown, who then introduced her to the rest of the class.

Laurie remembered how awkward it felt being the new kid when she moved to Compton. Thank goodness she'd met Howard before the first day of school so she was able to recognize a friendly face. She raised her hand.

"Yes, Laurie?" Ms. Brown asked.

"Carlotta can sit here." Laurie gestured to the empty desk next to her. "We've already met. We're neighbors."

"Thank you, Laurie, that would be wonderful," Ms. Brown answered. Then she turned her smile on Carlotta. "You'll know where to find every basketball hoop in Compton by the end of the week."

The class laughed good-naturedly. Carlotta grinned at

Howard and Laurie as she made her way to her seat.

There was no opportunity for conversation until lunch time. Laurie and Howard led Carlotta to their favorite table in the cafeteria, where Li joined them. Laurie opened her mouth to ask Carlotta why her family had left New York City, but Howard beat her to it.

"Was your old neighborhood dangerous?" he asked. "Drug dealers on every corner?"

Carlotta giggled. "Don't believe everything you hear about the big city. Our building was great. Nice people and everybody helped everyone else. I even had four cousins to hang out with."

"So why'd you leave?" Laurie managed to say before Howard could.

"My father's job," Carlotta explained. "He works nights, and commuting would take too long. We'd never see him."

"What does your father do?" Li asked.

"He's a shortstop like me," Carlotta beamed. "He's going to play for the Renegades."

Howard choked on his milk, and Laurie had to whack him on the back.

"The Hudson Valley Renegades are my favorite team!" Howard shouted. "Is your father Lorenzo Sanchez?"

"That's him. But how do you know his name? The season hasn't even started yet."

"The Renegades' web site has the team roster," Howard answered, tapping his laptop for emphasis. "Lorenzo Sanchez is supposed to be a big star for them."

"He plays a sweet shortstop, if I say so myself," Carlotta said.

"And he's teaching me everything he knows."

"Then I'll bet you'll be a shoo-in for shortstop," Howard said matter-of-factly.

Laurie wondered if she herself would be a shoo-in for anything.

Playing the Field

When the school day finally ended, Howard shot out of his seat and raced for the softball field. Laurie smiled. She knew he would have the equipment ready when the team arrived for practice.

Laurie walked Carlotta to her locker. Carlotta crammed her books inside and pulled her mitt and a baseball cap from the top shelf. Then they stopped by Laurie's locker to pick up her gear. Laurie had borrowed Howard's mitt, and her dad had given her a Cyclones' baseball cap at breakfast that morning. She slapped the cap on her head and tucked the mitt under her arm.

Outside, when the girls rounded the corner of the building, Carlotta spotted the diamond and took off running.

"Race you!" she cried over her shoulder to Laurie.

Laurie sprinted after her and stopped when she reached the field, a step behind Carlotta. But Carlotta kept right on going, until she stood at shortstop. Then she began cleaning pebbles off the infield.

"Looks like Carlotta really wants to play shortstop," said Li, her fingers wrapped around the wire mesh of the backstop.

"And she's not afraid to let anyone know," Laurie added.

The girls paired up on the sidelines to play catch while they waited for Coach Preston. Carlotta wouldn't leave the shortstop position, so Li joined her on the field. Laurie was partners with Luisa "Wheezy" Lopez, who spent as much time sneezing from the pollen in the spring air as she did catching and throwing. Sneezing or not, Laurie thought Wheezy looked happy to be surrounded by her friends and teammates.

In a few minutes, Coach Preston pulled up in his Jeep. Laurie called Carlotta over so she could introduce her. Carlotta seemed reluctant to leave the shortstop position unguarded, but at last she placed her mitt on the ground to mark her territory and trotted in.

"Dad, this is our new neighbor, Carlotta Sanchez. Her dad plays for the Renegades."

"It's a pleasure to meet you, Carlotta," Coach Preston said, shaking her hand. "I hope you will get to love Compton as much as Laurie and I do."

"Thanks, Coach," Carlotta said, then she quickly added, "I play shortstop."

"I'll be trying several players at each position, but I'll remember what you said," he promised.

"Once you see me play short, you won't need to see anyone else," Carlotta said with a smile.

"Boy, is she cocky," Laurie thought. But her dad didn't seem to mind Carlotta's confidence. He just grinned and called the rest of the team over.

Coach Preston briefly outlined the practice schedule before getting down to business. "We'll start with some hitting.

Returning players, stay in and bat. New players, take the field."

Carlotta was like a runner exploding from the starting blocks. Before anyone else had taken a step, she was back at shortstop, pounding her fist in her glove and smoothing the dirt with her sneakers.

Li grabbed Laurie's elbow and said, "Let's shag some flies. The outfield positions are wide open. Last year's starters are on the high-school team now."

Laurie put her hand in Howard's mitt and followed Li to the outfield. They joined basketball teammates Wheezy, Maggie Visosevic, and Angela Carillo.

"Hi, Laurie! Hi, Li!" Angela called, looking as peppy as ever. She bounced up and down and whirled her throwing arm.

"I am glad you came, Laurie," Maggie called. "You will love softball. It was my favorite sport when I lived in Croatia."

Maggie and her parents had fled war-torn Croatia and arrived in Compton not long before Laurie and her dad had moved to the town from upstate New York. Laurie remembered how Maggie had opened up and begun to fit in once she'd joined the basketball squad.

Laurie smiled, happy to be around her teammates again. "There's nothing like being on a team to make you feel like you belong," Laurie thought, feeling better about trying out for softball.

Coach Preston whistled and waved his arms for the girls to spread out. He was standing on the pitcher's mound, ready to start batting practice. Maggie and Wheezy trotted over to right field. Angela moved to left. Laurie and Li stayed in center. Two other basketball teammates, Eileen Riley and Jesse Jones, stood at first and third.

The first batter was star pitcher Dawn Adams. Dawn had a fluid swing that sent line drives sailing toward the outfield. Laurie had trouble judging the first two or three balls that came her way. They either landed in front of her or sailed over her head. But as her eye improved, she learned to track the flight of each ball and quickly position herself to make the catch. Soon her eye was so good, she ranged farther and farther across the outfield grass to race for Dawn's line drives, often beating Li to the ball.

Each time there was a grounder to short or second, Laurie raced in to back up the infielders. But they didn't need much help because Carlotta swept up everything that came her way. After her third backhanded play, Coach Preston pointed a finger at her.

"Shortstop," he announced.

Carlotta beamed.

Laurie got a lot more business backing up the player on second, a seventh grader named Emily Banks.

"They tell me she's a good hitter," Li said quietly as she and Laurie waited for some action, "but her fielding is terrible. Her errors cost the Cyclones two games last season."

When Jackie Morgan, the team's cleanup hitter, came to bat, Laurie had a blast. Jackie hit towering fly balls deep into the outfield. Laurie raced across the grass, her cap shielding her eyes from the sun, her gaze locked on the soaring ball. Laurie's good hands from basketball helped, too. Any ball she could reach, she caught. And she loved whipping long throws back to the infield. She was a natural ball hawk.

By the time the returning players were done hitting, Laurie was glad she had gone out for softball. As she ran in to take her swings, she called out, "You were right, Dad. This is fun."

Coach Preston grinned. "I thought you'd think so. Dig into that duffle bag at the end of the bench."

Laurie reached into the bag and pulled out a brand-new mitt. Written on the pocket was the signature *Dot Richardson*. She showed it to Howard.

"It's a beauty, Laurie," he said, twisting the stiff leather with his hands.

"Who's Dot Richardson?"

"She led the women's team to the Olympic gold medal," Howard answered. "Just like you'll lead us to the championship." He grinned at her.

Laurie handed Howard his mitt with a mumbled thanks, and he trotted out to the shortstop position left vacant by Carlotta. This was just what Laurie was afraid of.

If Howard expected miracles from her because of how great she was at basketball, maybe everyone would.

Home Run Cut

But Laurie didn't have time to worry. It was the newcomers' turn to take batting practice. Li would be the first batter to face Dawn.

"You're on deck, Laurie," Coach Preston said, coming over

to watch from the bench. Then he turned and yelled to Jackie, "Ten swings and then a bunt."

Laurie swung a bat in the on-deck circle while Li took her cuts. Li crouched low and choked up on the bat. She had a tiny strike zone, but Dawn threw pitch after pitch right over the heart of the plate. Li spanked the ball sharply, several of her hits skidding past the infielders. After her tenth swing, she lay down a bunt and hustled toward first base.

Now it was Laurie's turn, and she couldn't wait to rock one. Dawn threw her a fat pitch, and Laurie swung hard. She popped it up to the infield. Howard stumbled around under it, but made the catch. Dawn lobbed another, and Laurie swung harder still. Another pop fly, this time right back to the pitcher's mound. Laurie felt her face redden.

"You can do it, Laurie!" Li yelled. The other girls cheered her on, too.

Li had meant to help, but knowing that everyone was watching her made Laurie swing even harder. She swung so hard at the next pitch that when she missed it, she fell flat on her back.

Laurie jumped up as if nothing had happened. But she might as well have taken her time. Jackie had her mask off and was laughing hysterically. Dawn held her sides, too broken up to pitch.

Laurie dusted herself off with as much dignity as she could muster and somehow made it through the remaining swings. She had never bunted before, and her bunt was too hard. It rolled to first base long before Laurie had time to reach the bag. She flopped on the grass in foul territory. She couldn't face her teammates or her father after how foolish she had looked. Laurie risked a glance at her dad. His eyes were on Carlotta, who was beginning her turn at bat.

Chapter 2

Game Face

Carlotta looked as if she had been born with a bat in her hands. She scraped the ground in the batter's box with her sneakers, digging little hollows for her feet so she was less likely to lose her balance if she took a good rip. Laurie wished she had thought of doing that.

Carlotta glared at Dawn, as if daring her to throw a pitch. Dawn looked amused, but Laurie noticed that she threw the ball twice as hard as she had before. Carlotta turned and bunted toward third base. The ball spun lazily down the line and stopped dead before it reached third. In a game, Carlotta's effort would have been a sure base hit. But in batting practice, a player wasn't supposed to bunt until she had taken ten full swings

"Hit away, Carlotta," Coach Preston called, swinging an imaginary bat. "Dawn, ease up a little," he added.

Dawn frowned and went back to lobbing the ball. She suddenly seemed unable to throw strikes. Carlotta was forced to take wild swings. She foul-tipped a few and missed some pitches completely. But Laurie didn't think Carlotta was embarrassed. She looked angry.

After ten full swings, Carlotta laid down a bunt that rolled slowly toward first. Dawn sprang from the mound. Her path took her across the base line. She bent to field the ball just as Carlotta came roaring down the line. The girls collided and rolled over, their bodies a tangle of arms and legs.

There might have been a scuffle, but Coach Preston and Jackie were on the spot before either girl could get up. Jackie grabbed Dawn and helped her to her feet. Coach Preston wrapped his arms around Carlotta, who scowled fiercely at Dawn.

"The base line is mine," Carlotta shouted.

"Chill, girl," Dawn snapped.

"Nobody makes me look bad on the diamond," Carlotta shot back.

"Both of you, calm down," Coach Preston ordered. He let go of Carlotta, but stood between the two girls. "Dawn, you know you didn't throw Carlotta the same quality pitches you threw the other girls."

Dawn started to protest, then lowered her gaze.

Coach Preston turned to his new shortstop. "Carlotta, control your temper or go sit on the bench. Now let's get back to work here."

Carlotta stopped at the bench long enough to grab her glove. Then she ran out to shortstop, waving Howard away from her position. Dawn shook her head and walked back to the mound. Laurie couldn't believe Carlotta had gotten so mad so fast. The only good thing was that the collision had taken everyone's mind off how foolish Laurie had looked lying in the dirt next to home plate.

Scrimmage

After batting practice, Coach Preston split the team into two squads for a scrimmage, mixing new and returning players on each side. He pitched for both teams, lobbing the ball into the strike zone.

Laurie studied the good hitters from her place in center field and realized that she had been swinging too hard. She decided to model herself after Li. Li stroked the ball, instead of swinging from her heels. When Laurie's turn at bat came, she smacked the ball sharply to third base. It wasn't a base hit, but it was a big improvement over her swings at batting practice.

Carlotta put on a show at shortstop, fielding balls that looked like sure base hits. She released the ball quickly, and Laurie could hear it smack into Eileen's glove at first base.

When Carlotta came to bat, she went through the same digging-in routine that had impressed Laurie earlier. Carlotta looked like a real hitter—then she squared around and bunted Coach Preston's first pitch. He called time before she had run halfway to first.

"Let's see you swing away, Carlotta. I know you're a good bunter, but you need to work on the rest of your offense."

Carlotta frowned, but came back to the plate. She swung at Coach Preston's softest lob and hit an easy pop-up to second base. Two innings later, she swung and missed twice before hitting a foul pop that Jackie easily handled.

"Let me bunt, Coach!" Carlotta shouted. "I know I can't hit. Why give my at bats away?"

"I've seen you bunt, and it's one of your strengths," Coach Preston answered, "but practice is for working on weaknesses, too."

Carlotta walked back to the bench, her shoulders drooping.

Despite Carlotta's batting troubles, each inning brought a bigger grin to Coach Preston's face. By the time practice ended, he was in a great mood. The girls gathered in a circle around the pitcher's mound.

"Great first practice, ladies. If we work as hard every day as we did today, there will be no stopping us this season. See you all tomorrow."

As the girls gathered up their gear, Laurie noticed Carlotta approach her dad, her head lowered.

"Sorry for being out of line, Coach," Laurie heard her say. "I just wanted to make a good impression at the first practice. You know, show everybody what I can do rather than what I can't do."

"No problem, Carlotta," Coach Preston said gently. "But you can't give up on your hitting. Your bunting will be more effective if you don't do it every time you bat."

As she watched Carlotta trot across the field to her parents' car, Laurie had to admit she understood Carlotta's behavior. She knew how embarrassing it was to play badly in front of everyone and how frustrating it was to try to improve.

"C'mon, gang. Let's head home." Coach Preston's voice broke into Laurie's thoughts.

Howard and Li clambered into the Jeep, chattering excitedly about the new season. As Laurie buckled her seat belt, she couldn't help but wonder what role she would play for the team. She and Li were both after the center field position. Laurie thought she was every bit as good as Li at running down fly balls, and she had a stronger throwing arm. But Li was a much better hitter. Laurie knew she would have to work on her stroke if she was going to win the starting job.

After Coach Preston had dropped off Li and Howard, Laurie turned to her father.

"Dad, you've got to help me with my hitting. What was I doing wrong out there?"

Coach Preston smiled. "Sounds like you're getting into softball already, Laurie."

"If I'm going to play, I want to be good. Help me."

"The first thing is patience. You can't expect to become a star overnight. I was amazed that you did so well in the field."

"But you will help me with my hitting, right?" Laurie persisted.

"Sure. You already figured out for yourself that you can't swing with all your might and expect to hit the ball. Now you have to learn the strike zone."

"Can we hit a few after supper?"

"By the time we've eaten and you've done your homework, it'll be dark. After practice tomorrow we'll sneak in a few extra minutes. I'm going to stop by the Sanchezes tonight and see if we can bring Carlotta home from practice so she can work on her batting, too. She needs the work more than you do."

He pulled up to their house and turned off the engine. "Don't worry," he said as he stepped outside. "You'll be hitting line drives before you know it."

"I'd be hitting them sooner if you'd help just me and not Carlotta, too," Laurie couldn't help thinking.

Assistant Coach

At the next practice, the team worked on bunting. Carlotta stood tall when Coach Preston chose her to demonstrate the proper technique.

"Softball games are won by teams that can move a runner up a base with a well-placed bunt, and lost by those that can't," he explained.

When Laurie's turn came, she managed to lay down three in a row without popping any in the air. She was feeling pretty good about herself when Carlotta's voice rang out.

"Softer, Laurie! Let the ball hit the bat. Don't jab at the ball."

Laurie felt her face grow warm. She looked to her dad, and he nodded his head at Carlotta, agreeing with her. How embarrassing! Laurie wished Carlotta had taken her aside to tell her instead of yelling it out in front of everyone. She believed in helping teammates improve, but Carlotta's advice irritated her.

During the scrimmage, Carlotta bunted every time she came to bat. When Carlotta rolled one down the first base line, Dawn took a little extra time to field the ball, and Carlotta beat the play. Laurie bet that yesterday's collision made Dawn hesitate today.

In her next at bat, Carlotta's bunt sent Jackie scrambling out from behind the plate. It was a tough play for a catcher, and Carlotta was such a speedy runner that Jackie couldn't afford to waste a second. Jackie picked up the bunt and threw the ball into right field. Carlotta sped all the way to third base.

When Carlotta came to the plate with the bases loaded, Coach Preston called out, "Let's see you swing at this one, Carlotta. You can do it." Carlotta nodded. But on the very first pitch, she squared and bunted into an easy force play.

Suddenly Laurie knew why getting advice from Carlotta rubbed her the wrong way. Carlotta seemed to know how everyone else could improve, but she didn't even try to overcome her own weakness. She was a terrible hitter, so all she did was bunt. She even ignored Coach Preston's orders to hit away. Why didn't Carlotta learn how to hit first, and then worry about helping her teammates?

While studying together that night, Laurie decided to talk to Li about Carlotta.

"It's obvious Carlotta knows a lot about the game," Li replied. "Everyone knows she's not a great hitter, but her weakness doesn't mean her advice is worthless. I think she really wants to help the team."

Laurie grudgingly agreed. Then she tried another tactic. "Well, then, how can she be so quiet and friendly off the field, and so aggressive on it?"

"Look at you," Li smiled.

"Me?!" She was stunned.

"In school, you let people ahead of you in line. But if someone tries to catch a fly ball that you think should be yours, she gets run over."

"You said that the center fielder rules the outfield," Laurie countered. "Any ball she can reach is hers as long as she calls for it."

"But when we're shagging flies, we're both center fielders," explained Li. "You call for balls before you're even sure you can get to them."

"When I miss one, let me know," Laurie retorted.

Li nudged Laurie with her elbow to show she was kidding. But Laurie could tell that she wasn't the only one worried about making the starting lineup. She wanted to be the starting center fielder, but why did it have to mean taking the job from Li?

For the rest of the week, Coach Preston worked with Laurie after practice, and Laurie felt that her hitting was improving. Against his lobs, she could drive the ball hard to any part of the field. There was just one problem: If Laurie stayed for extra batting practice, that meant so did Li, since Coach Preston drove her home, too. Laurie couldn't figure out how she was going to catch up to Li, if Li worked just as hard as she did.

Carlotta stayed late as well, but the extra practice didn't help her improve her batting. Coach Preston tried having her choke up on the bat. He had her stand closer to the plate. Li suggested that she hit from a crouch. Nothing seemed to help. Laurie felt sorry for Carlotta, but she couldn't help but be happy that there was one player on the team that she could out hit.

Starting Lineup

Laurie stood in center field on a warm April afternoon and watched Dawn throw her warm-up pitches. There was only one week to go before the season opener, and her father still hadn't named a starting lineup.

She looked around at her teammates. Dawn and Jackie were sure things as pitcher and catcher. Jesse was solid at third base and was a decent pitcher, too. Carlotta, of course, was a fantastic shortstop. Eileen was great at digging throws out of the dirt. She was bound to play first base. Those were the players Laurie knew would start.

It looked like second base was going to be a weak spot. When Dawn finished her warmups, Jackie threw the ball down to Emily at second. The throw was a little low, and it skipped by her. Laurie ran in to get it. Maybe Emily would do enough good with her bat to make up for the harm she did with her glove.

Most important to Laurie was who would play the outfield. Li, Maggie, Wheezy, and Angela were all competing with her for the three spots. Wheezy was having a hard time with her asthma, as she did every spring. She would probably be satisfied being a part-time player. But Laurie knew that the other three really wanted to start.

The rest of the girls out for the team didn't seem to be a threat to break into the lineup. They were as inexperienced as Laurie, but they lacked her athletic ability.

The batter sent one of Dawn's lob pitches soaring into left center field. Laurie was off at the crack of the bat. She raced across the grass, each stride taking her farther into the outfield. At the last second, she leaped and speared the ball, turning a potential RBI double into a harmless out. Angela, who trailed the play, let out a whoop.

Laurie's heart pounded. She hoped her dad hadn't missed that catch. Wouldn't he want her in center when she could save the team runs? Wasn't that as good as knocking them in with her bat?

With three outs, Laurie's team ran in to bat. Laurie passed Li on her way to the bench. Li waved her glove to draw Laurie's attention. Laurie thought she was just being friendly, so she returned the wave but continued off the field. She squeezed in next to Howard on the bench.

"Great catch, Laurie," Howard said. "What do you think of the experiment?"

Laurie gave Howard a puzzled look, so he pointed to the diamond. Li was playing second base. That's why she had tried to get Laurie's attention. Laurie's pulse began to race. If Li played second, Laurie could have the center field job. Maybe they could both be starters after all.

"Has she ever played second base before?" Laurie asked.

"She told your dad it was her regular position in Little League. She only tried out for center because she thought there was an opening there."

"What about Emily?" Laurie said quietly, since Emily was a few feet away in the on-deck circle.

Howard shrugged. "No big deal. She can be the designated hitter."

Laurie hadn't realized that there could be a designated hitter, a player who batted but never played the field, in softball. That meant someone else would play the field but not bat. For a moment she panicked, thinking how she would hate to be the player left out of the batting order. Then she remembered

Carlotta. Thank goodness Carlotta was such a weak hitter. Laurie was sure her dad would leave Carlotta out of the lineup.

A few minutes later, Li got a chance to show her skills at second base. Laurie was batting with a runner on base and two outs. Jesse lobbed a ball on the outside corner, and Laurie met it cleanly. She hit a hard smash that seemed headed into right center for a base hit.

But Li snared the ball in the webbing of her glove and flipped it to first base for the out that ended the inning. Laurie didn't know whether to be disappointed that she'd been robbed of a hit or glad that Li was showing she belonged at second base.

Double Play

On the ride home, everyone buzzed with excitement.

"Thanks for the chance at second base, Coach," Li said.

"Our infield is going to be great," Carlotta remarked. "With Dawn's pitching and our fielding, we'll shut those other teams down."

Laurie had to ask, "Is the center field job mine, Dad?"

"You're a great fielder, Laurie," Coach Preston replied. "If anyone does manage to hit the ball past my all-star infield, you're the one I want out there."

A wide smile spread across Laurie's face. Carlotta and Li high-fived her.

Howard was banging away on his laptop keyboard. "Our fielding stats have been down, but they'll go through the roof now."

"I think you're right, Howard," Coach Preston said happily.

After dinner, Laurie was helping Grandma Preston with the dishes when the doorbell rang. "That's going to be Li and Carlotta," she said. "They're coming over to study." She put the last dish in the cupboard and went to greet her friends.

"How's the double-play combo?" Laurie asked, as the girls slipped off their sneakers and hung up their coats.

"We can't wait to work together," Carlotta enthused. "I hope your father puts us on the same team in the scrimmages from now on."

"Me, too," Li agreed.

"Girls, can you come in here?" Grandma's voice called from the kitchen. "I have a favor to ask now that you're all together."

"Favor?" Laurie wondered. What was her grandmother up to? The girls found Grandma dishing up bowls of ice cream, and they eagerly accepted her invitation to dig in.

Grandma waited until everyone had had a chance to eat a few spoonfuls. Then she spoke.

"A good friend of mine, Sally Carnovski, lost her husband last year," she began. "She's been moping around the house. She used to be a great gardener, but she's not strong enough to do it by herself any more."

"What can we do?" Carlotta asked between mouthfuls.

"Would you be willing to go over to her place on Saturdays and help out? I just know that she'd be much happier if she could get her hands into the soil again."

Laurie made eye contact with Li and Carlotta. Li shrugged her shoulders as if saying, "Why not?" Carlotta grinned.

"We'll be glad to, Grandma," Laurie said. "And I bet Howard will come, too. The only thing is, I don't know much about gardening."

"I do," Carlotta piped up. "When we visit my Grandma Sanchez in Puerto Rico, I always help her garden."

Grandma smiled. "I knew I could count on you. There's just one thing."

"What's that?" Laurie asked, a little warily.

"Sally has arthritis. She can't get around like she used to, and it's made her a little cranky. But if you give her a chance, I think you'll find that you have a lot in common."

"Don't worry about us," Laurie said. "We're used to cranks. Dad's our coach."

"I heard that!" Coach Preston yelled from the next room. He popped his head through the kitchen doorway and said with mock severity, "I should bench you, Laurie Bird Preston."

Laurie threw up her hands. "See, Grandma?" And the three friends collapsed into giggles.

Final Prep

With opening day drawing near, Coach Preston began to play his starters as a unit. Each day Laurie played center with Maggie in right and Angela in left. The two girls were steady hitters, but only average fielders, which was fine with Laurie. Their weaknesses allowed her to pursue batted balls more often.

The Cyclones' infield defense was airtight. Jesse at third and Eileen at first had great hands. Carlotta had phenomenal range and a sensational throwing arm. Li was quick and agile. Her weak arm wasn't a problem because she never had to make a long throw from second base.

Standing in center Laurie had a great viewpoint from which to admire her friends' sparkling play. And with lob pitching still the rule, many of the hitters knocked out long line drives and deep fly balls, so she had plenty of opportunities to show off her own skills in center field. She couldn't wait for the season to start.

During the extra practices, Laurie began making solid contact at bat. Coach Preston began working on her knowledge of the strike zone. When he pitched to her, he called each pitch a strike or a ball. Laurie found his advice more annoying than helpful. If she could reach a pitch, she wanted to swing at it. What fun was hitting if you just stood there and watched the ball go by?

"Ball!" Coach Preston barked at her one evening, after she'd reached out and slashed a pitch between first and second.

"A base hit beats a ball any day, Dad," she shouted impatiently. "If I can hit the ball, I've got to try."

"Swing at bad pitches, and bad pitches are all you'll get to hit."

"What's the difference, Dad, as long as I hit them?"

"It's not that simple," he sighed. "If you swing at a pitch that's a little outside, the next one will be farther off the plate. You're helping the pitcher out too much."

Laurie could see that her father was worried. "I'll try, Dad. It's just that I want to do well and help the team. Sometimes I have to wait three innings for my turn to hit. It's a waste to go up looking for a walk."

Laurie thought of Carlotta. Carlotta started every at bat by taking one strike. Then she would bunt. When she got on, she was a great base runner. But now that the infielders had learned to play in close against her, she didn't get on base very often.

Laurie wondered if her dad thought the opponents would catch on to Carlotta's batting routine, too. Surely he'd see that Laurie's determination to hit pitches would help the team more than Carlotta's predictable at bats.

Chapter 3

Grounds Crew

On Saturday, Howard rang the doorbell before Laurie had taken a bite of her pancakes. Grandma invited Howard to join them, and when he and Laurie were stuffed, they walked over to Carlotta's house.

When Carlotta opened the door, she took one look at Howard's eager expression and shook her head. "I'm sorry, Howard, but my father left already. The Renegades have to get ready for their opener, too, you know."

"What fun is it living near a professional ball player when you never get to see the guy?" Howard sighed. "Good thing it's a long season."

They walked down the sunny streets, talking and laughing. Howard sorted through a new pack of baseball cards, so engrossed that he nearly walked into a mailbox. As arranged, they met Li along the way. Laurie checked the directions her grandmother had given her. She led the group right for two blocks and then left for one more. The houses on this street had large yards and neatly trimmed bushes lining the driveways. At the end of the block was Mrs. Carnovski's white, two-storied house.

Laurie rang the doorbell.

"All right! The Octopus!" Howard shouted, holding up a card. "Do you guys know how he got that nickname?"

"Is his skin covered with suction cups?" Li asked.

"Even cooler. He's got six fingers on each hand!" Howard shouted.

Li pretended to gag. Carlotta said, "*Pulpo*—that's his Spanish nickname. My dad says he's got six toes on each foot also."

"Hey, Li, slap me six!" Howard teased, waving one hand and the index finger of his other.

Laurie giggled, then decided to ring the bell again. Grandma had said that Mrs. Carnovski was old. Maybe she was hard of hearing.

Just as she pushed the button, the door was yanked open. Laurie jumped back. A stooped figure slowly emerged and a raspy voice croaked, "I'm coming! I'm coming!"

"Mrs. Carnovski," Laurie began, recovering herself, "I'm Laurie Preston."

"Then your grandmother is the one that came up with this bird-brained idea," snapped Mrs. Carnovski. "Well, you're going to have to be a lot more patient than you were just now if you're going to work with me."

She stopped talking long enough to include Howard, Li, and Carlotta in her glare. "It takes me a while to get places, but I'm not deaf. Ring the bell once and I'll come. Understand?"

Laurie was starting to regret volunteering. She thought the others must have felt the same way. Howard stepped forward.

"Howard Goldstein, Mrs. Car—"

"Just Mrs. C, Howard," she interrupted. "Who are your friends?"

"Carlotta Sanchez," Carlotta said, smoothing her hair.

"Li Tang, Mrs. C," Li said.

"Well, at least you showed up on time. Now if you're sure you want to do some work, meet me around back. I'll walk through the house." She started to close the door, then added, "And don't expect me to beat you back there."

When the door slammed shut, Laurie turned to the others. "What did we get ourselves into?" she moaned.

"If we run for it, we can be halfway home before she figures out we've left," Carlotta teased.

"Let's give her a chance," Li said. "If she's friends with your grandma, Laurie, she can't be all bad."

"Grandma claims we have a lot in common," Laurie said as they walked slowly around Mrs. C's house.

"What a horrible thing to say about anyone," Howard joked.

While they waited for Mrs. C, they looked over the overgrown garden. It was full of tangled, matted dead plants. A mummified pumpkin disintegrated into a cloud of dust when Howard prodded it with the toe of his sneaker. The new season's weeds were the only touch of green.

"If staring at it would clean it up, I wouldn't need you kids," squawked Mrs. C, causing all four of them to jump. She leaned on her cane with one arm and handed Howard a key.

"This will open the tool shed. The first step is to go in the shed and get me a folding chair before this foolish cane sinks so far into the ground that I'm down on all fours."

Laurie and Howard opened the shed door. Inside, all was in order. Every type of garden tool hung on the wall. Laurie found a folding chair. She dusted it off with her sleeve and brought it to Mrs. C. The old woman didn't say thanks, but when Laurie saw the effort it took for her to settle herself into the chair, she couldn't blame her for being cranky.

Howard brought out a wheelbarrow filled with an assortment of rakes and hoes. The four friends set to work while Mrs. C dozed in the spring sunshine. When all the dead plants and weeds had been removed, they didn't know what to do next.

Luckily Coach Preston arrived just then. His booming hello woke Mrs. C, who jerked herself straight in her chair. Coach Preston introduced himself and explained that he had come to take lunch orders. Grandma Preston was going to make sandwiches for everyone.

"No sandwich for me, thanks," Mrs. C croaked. "I've got to watch my waistline now that I don't get much exercise."

Laurie looked around the large lawn that separated the house and garden. She swallowed hard and said, "Mrs. C, would it be all right if we threw a ball around on our lunch break? Dad could bring our equipment when he brings the sandwiches. Our first game is on Monday, and we want to stay sharp."

"Oh, you're ball players, are you? Just my luck," she cackled. "Who pays for the broken windows?"

"Mrs. Carnovski, my players have too much control of their game to do any damage," Coach Preston assured her.

"We'll see," said Mrs. C said suspiciously, but Laurie thought she saw the hint of a smile on the old woman's face.

Pepperpot

By the time Coach Preston returned with sandwiches and a Thermos of lemonade, the four friends were hot and thirsty. Mrs. C had sent them back into the shed for a screen, and they had sifted the rich, dark soil with it, breaking up the lumps and removing any rocks.

"You kids did a great job," Coach Preston said, looking at Mrs. C for confirmation.

"They're good workers," she conceded, "as long as I keep an eye on them."

Laurie had to stifle a laugh. Mrs. C had dozed off again, not waking up until the job was done.

The friends used the garden hose to wash their hands and sat down on the grass to eat. Coach Preston had left a duffle bag full of equipment before leaving to run some errands.

Laurie was surprised that Mrs. C had turned her chair so that she could watch them unload the softball equipment.

"You guys want to play pepper?" Carlotta asked.

"How do you play?" Li asked.

"It's fun," Carlotta assured them, "and easy. Line up side by side and face the house, and I'll show you."

Carlotta grabbed a bat while Laurie, Li, and Howard pulled on gloves. Howard stood in the middle with Li on one side and Laurie on the other. Carlotta faced them and backed about ten feet away. She flipped a softball to Laurie.

"Pitch the ball, and I have to try and hit it past you. Field anything you can get and toss it back. If I hit one in the air and you catch it, it's your turn to bat."

The game started slowly, but within a few minutes there was a fast-paced volley of grounders and throws. Soon the smack of the ball hitting the gloves, the thunk of ball against bat, and the players' laughter filled the air.

Carlotta finally popped one up. Howard bobbled it, but caught it before it hit the ground. He whooped happily and ran in for his turn at bat. Carlotta grabbed his mitt and joined the line.

Howard hit a weak grounder that Laurie snared. She tossed it back. Howard must have decided that he wasn't swinging hard enough, because he ripped the ball. It looked like it was headed toward the birdbath near the garden, but Carlotta threw herself sideways and speared it on the first hop.

Mrs. C yelled, "That's the way to play, baby!" and banged her cane against the metal frame of her chair.

Laurie and Li stared at each other with dropped jaws.

Howard didn't want to hit anymore after his near disaster, so Laurie took his place. She had only batted for a minute when she tried to hit a high throw from Howard and popped it straight in the air. Li gathered it in easily.

As Laurie and Li traded spots, Mrs. C called out, "Your father's a coach, and he hasn't taught you to lay off the wild ones? What's the game coming to?"

While Li batted, Laurie seethed. Was there anyone who didn't think they knew more about softball than she did? She expected her father to correct her. He was her coach. But Carlotta had no business giving advice when she herself couldn't hit. And now an old woman thought she was a softball expert. What a joke!

Wily Veteran

"What's next, Mrs. C?" Carlotta asked when it was time to go back to work.

"To tell you the truth, that's about it for this week," Mrs. C said. "I'll have my seeds and everything else by next Saturday, if you can come back."

"We'll be here," Howard promised, but Carlotta shook her head.

"Next Saturday is my father's home opener," she began.

"Home opener?" asked Mrs. C.

"Her dad's the shortstop for the Renegades," Howard explained.

"No wonder you're such a slick fielder," Mrs. C said, causing Carlotta to smile.

Laurie was annoyed. Carlotta got praise, while she got criticism.

"I guess we'll go then," Laurie said.

"If you're not in a hurry," said Mrs. C, "there is one job inside the house I could use help with."

"What are we? Her personal servants?" Laurie thought.

But Li said, "Sure, Mrs. C, we'll do it."

Mrs. C heaved herself out of the chair. "I'll start walking in while you put the tools and my chair away. By the time you get the shed locked, I'll be up on the second floor. Meet me there."

The girls carried the tools to Howard, who hung them back in place in the shed. Laurie looked to make sure Mrs. C had made it back to the house. Then she said, "Don't you think she's taking advantage of us? We offered to help with the garden, and now she's got us working inside, too."

"I think she wants us to hang around for a while," Li reasoned. "She's lonely."

"It won't take long, Laurie," Howard chimed in. "Mrs. C must be about due for another nap. We'll be out of here before you know it."

"I kind of like her," Carlotta added.

"Sure, she's nice to you," Laurie muttered.

When they reached the second floor, Mrs. C was leaning on her cane and waiting. She pointed to a rope hanging from a trap door in the ceiling.

"I need something from the attic, and I'm too old to climb the steps. You're the tallest, Carlotta. Pull that door down."

Carlotta tugged the rope. The door opened and Laurie saw a folded flight of steps attached to it. She reached up and extended the steps so that they touched the floor.

"There should be a brown trunk up there," Mrs. C said, handing Laurie a flashlight. "You all go up and drag it over near the door. Take the things out of the trunk and bring them down here."

With Laurie leading the way, they scrambled up the steps. Laurie shone the beam around the attic. Against the far wall she spotted the trunk. She and Carlotta each grabbed one of the handles on the ends and pulled. It barely moved. Howard and Li grabbed hold, too, and with much grunting and straining, they all maneuvered it next to the trap door.

Laurie wondered what was inside. Probably clothes that

went out of style fifty years ago or something equally boring.

She pulled back the lid to find a faded baseball cap on top of a stack of magazines and newspapers. The friends looked at one another with wide eyes. Laurie put the cap on her head and grabbed one of the yellowed newspapers. She cast the beam of the flashlight on it and read the headline: HOT ROD LEADS THE WAY. Underneath was a blurry photo of a catcher whipping a throw to second base. Had Mr. Carnovski been a baseball player?

Li, Howard, and Carlotta pulled out the papers and magazines and set them carefully on the floor. Laurie shone the beam into the trunk and found an ancient wool jersey with ROCKFORD stitched across the chest in bright red letters. She held it up for the others to see.

Howard called, "Mrs. C, was your husband a ball player?"

The only answer was a raucous laugh.

Laurie's jaw dropped as she unfolded the uniform. The jersey flared out into a skirt. The friends scooted over to the trap door, poked their heads through, and stared at Mrs. C.

"I'm the Hot Rod, all right!" she cackled, delighted at the sight of the four astonished faces.

Old Timer's Day

Laurie had seen *A League of Their Own*, a movie about the All-American Girls Professional Baseball League in the 1940s. But she never dreamed she'd actually meet one of the players. They hauled the memorabilia down the stairs and into Mrs. C's sunny kitchen. There they sat around the table, drinking lemonade and taking turns reading the newspaper articles aloud.

Howard had his hand in an old, flat catcher's mitt, a dazed but happy look on his face. Carlotta wore the Rockford uniform over her T-shirt and shorts while she and Li leafed through a battered yearbook.

Each clipping brought back a memory for Mrs. C. Laurie held up a story with a headline that read HOT ROD RUNS WILD.

"We were playing in Racine, Wisconsin, on a beautiful Saturday afternoon, and the stands were packed. Racine had a tricky left-handed pitcher named Jensen, and we couldn't do anything with her. Then I noticed that every time she pitched, she fell toward the third base line.

"So when it was my turn to bat, I pushed a bunt just to the first base side of the pitcher's mound. Jensen couldn't get it. The girls playing first and second both charged the ball, which left nobody to cover first base. I could have walked to the bag!"

Mrs. C cackled.

"The best part was that Jensen was so mad that she kept throwing over to first, trying to pick me off. I danced around a little to agitate her, and she whipped a throw way over the first baseman's head. I was off like a flash. The coach waved me on, so I tried for third base. Would you believe the ball skipped through the third baseman's legs and I scored standing up? Only run of the game," Mrs. C sighed with satisfaction.

When Li looked at her watch, everyone was shocked to see that it was four o'clock. They thanked Mrs. C for the lemonade and the stories and got ready to leave. Laurie was a little ashamed that she'd felt resentful when Mrs. C had tried to give her advice. Grandma was right—they did have a lot in common.

When they reached the front door, Laurie turned back. "Mrs. C, we have a home game Monday after school. My grandmother will be going. I'm sure she'll bring you along—if you don't mind watching a bunch of kids play."

"I'll be there!" she squawked. "The Hot Rod rides again!"

Opening Day

On Monday, the Belair Bobcats' bus pulled up in front of Compton Middle School. The Cyclones were on the field taking their pregame warmups. And warmups was the correct term. The weather, which had been sunny and mild for a week, had taken a drastic turn for the worse. The sky was filled with clouds, and a chilly wind swept across the field. Laurie thought it felt more like November than April.

Laurie bounced up and down on the balls of her feet as she waited for her dad to hit a fungo her way. She wheeled her throwing arm around, trying to keep her shoulder loose. She and Li had warmed up earlier, but her arm had stiffened in the cold.

The Bobcats filed off the bus and were soon ready to take the field. Coach Preston waved his players in and gathered them in a circle behind the bench. Howard was copying the lineup into the score book, and Laurie was dying to see which names he was writing down. She was afraid she would bat last, which would be disappointing. But the way she had been stinging the ball in practice lately, she was confident she could work her way up the batting order.

"Ladies," Coach Preston began, "you've worked hard and you're ready. Stay alert, play hard, and have fun."

He looked over his shoulder and lowered his voice.

"Here are the signs. If I tip my cap," he lifted his cap and ran his fingers through his hair, "that means take, let the pitch go by. Both hands on the belt means bunt. You're free to bunt whenever you think you can beat one out for a hit, but if I grab my belt with both hands, you have to bunt the next pitch, no matter where it's thrown."

Laurie caught her dad making eye contact with Carlotta to make sure she understood the signs. For the first time, Laurie began to feel uneasy. She had assumed Carlotta would play shortstop but that Emily, the designated hitter, would bat in her place. If Carlotta was in the batting order, who was left out?

"Skin on skin means steal." Coach Preston rubbed his hands on his face, then rubbed them together to show another way he might give the sign. Then he turned to Howard.

"Howard, give the team the batting order. I've got to meet with Coach Scott and the umpires about the ground rules."

Howard read from the score book.

"Li, Emily, Dawn, Jackie, Jesse, Eileen, Angela, Maggie, and Carlotta." Howard glanced over at Laurie, but avoided her eyes. "Laurie, you're playing center, but Emily's batting in your spot."

Laurie felt tears well in her eyes. How could her father do this to her? Carlotta was a terrible hitter, but she was in the batting order and Laurie was left out. Laurie was still trying to adjust to the news when the Bobcats ran in. It was time for the Cyclones to take the field.

Chapter 4

Left-Out Laurie

Laurie didn't trust herself to go near Carlotta. She ran in front of the pitcher's mound and then out past second base to reach her position. Li squeezed her arm and wished her luck as she passed by, but Laurie was too numb to respond.

She supposed she must have tossed the warm-up ball around the outfield with Angela and Maggie, but the next thing she knew, the home plate umpire was yelling, "Batter up!" and the game was about to begin.

Laurie forced herself to focus on the action. If she messed up a play in the field, her father would probably bench her.

For the first time Laurie saw Dawn pitch without holding anything back, and it was an impressive sight. The Belair lead-off batter took two fastballs that split the plate for strikes, then swung at and missed another fastball, which had zoomed in at shoulder height. Before the Belair player realized she was out, Jackie had snapped a throw to Jesse at third, and the Cyclones were whipping the ball around the infield.

Laurie remembered her duties as center fielder and yelled, "One out," first to Maggie, then to Angela. They each held up one finger to signal that they understood, and Laurie turned back to the infield.

Dawn retired the next two batters on easy grounders, and Laurie ran for the bench with her teammates. There was polite applause from the fans, and rising over it, a squawk that drew Laurie's attention.

"Come on, Cyclones! Let's get some runs."

Mrs. C was sitting in a lawn chair close behind the Cyclones' bench. Laurie was humiliated that Mrs. C would see that she wasn't good enough to even bat last.

Laurie wanted to know if anyone else thought she belonged in the batting order instead of Carlotta. Li might have been sympathetic, but she was leading off. Howard was stationed in the third-base coaching box. Angela and Maggie sat on either side of Carlotta, so there was no way Laurie could complain to them. Wheezy was using her inhaler to fight off the pollen from the budding trees that surrounded the Compton diamond.

Mrs. C's voice boomed. Laurie looked up to see Li trotting to first base. She had started the inning by drawing a walk. Emily was next. She struck out swinging on a ball in the dirt, but Li was running on the pitch. By the time the catcher scooped up the ball and threw it, Li had stolen second. When Dawn followed with a clean single, the Cyclones had the lead.

Laurie jumped up and joined her teammates in congratulating Li on scoring the first run of the season. Then she followed Li back to the bench. At last she could tell Li how she felt. But before she could begin, there was a groan from the fans. Jackie Morgan had hit into a double play, ending the inning.

By the time Dawn had retired the side again, Laurie had decided not to say anything to anyone until after the game. A drizzle was falling, chilling the players to the bone. It wouldn't be fair to add another distraction in the middle of a game.

Most of the fans, including Grandma Preston, had taken shelter in their cars and were watching the action from there. Mrs. C turned up the collar on her jacket and stayed put. "I want to keep an eye on this ump and make sure he does a good job," she said in a voice loud enough for the umpire to hear.

The score remained 1 to 0 into the last inning. The game was tense and exciting, but Laurie felt more like a spectator than a player. Dawn was pitching so well that not a single ball had come to center field. The Bobcats' few hard hits were grounders, and most of those were snared by Li or Carlotta.

As Laurie took the field, she wanted nothing more than the game to end. She was cold, wet, and miserable. The cold may have gotten to Dawn, too, for she suddenly lost her control. She walked the first batter on four pitches. The Bobcats' cleanup hitter was next, so Laurie backed up a few steps. No sooner had she taken her deeper position, then the batter hit a little looper off the handle of the bat.

Laurie charged in at full speed, not sure she could reach the ball. Three more strides and she knew she could snag it before it hit the ground. She yelled, "Mine!" at the top of her lungs. At the same instant, Carlotta called for the ball. But after waiting all day, Laurie wasn't going to pass up this opportunity. She kept charging. Carlotta got plenty of chances to show off. This was Laurie's turn.

Still yelling, Laurie bent to field the ball. Just as it hit her glove, Carlotta ran into her. The girls tumbled to the ground, the ball squirting loose. Luckily, Li was nearby. As Laurie fought to untangle herself from Carlotta, she saw Li grab the ball and run it back to the infield. But the Bobcats now had runners on first and third.

Coach Preston called time and ran out to Laurie and Carlotta.

"I had the ball," Laurie snarled, glaring at Carlotta.

"We both called for it," Carlotta snapped back. "I wasn't sure you could get there."

"The damage is done now," Coach Preston pointed out. "If you're both okay, let's play ball."

Laurie turned her back on Carlotta and trotted back to her position. "What a ball hog!" she thought.

Coach Preston walked back to the infield, stopping at the mound to talk to Dawn. Laurie paced back and forth in center, more restless by the minute.

"At least in basketball, when there's a time-out everyone hears what the coach is saying," she sulked to herself. "I'm so far from the action, it's like I'm not even on the team."

Whatever Coach Preston said must have helped Dawn. The next batter popped up to Jackie in front of home plate. Laurie added her cheer to her teammates' and reminded her fellow outfielders to throw the ball home if a Bobcat hit a fly ball.

Dawn worked the count to two balls and two strikes on the following hitter. Then she tried to sneak a changeup past her. The batter smashed a hard grounder up the middle of the diamond. Laurie charged in, praying she wouldn't lose her footing on the wet grass. Then Carlotta dove.

It seemed that the ball had gone by her, but somehow Carlotta snared it her glove's webbing. As she skidded across the ground, she flipped the ball toward second base. Li had sped toward the bag the instant the ball was struck. She found the base with her left foot and caught Carlotta's flip for the force-out.

The Bobcats cheered as the tying run scored. The Cyclones cheered Carlotta's great play. Laurie forgot her hurt feelings for a moment and cheered as loudly as anyone—anyone except Mrs. C, that is.

Muddy, but grinning, Carlotta took her position at short. Dawn fanned the next batter, and the Cyclones ran off the field.

Slide

Before taking his place in the coaching box at first, Coach Preston patted Carlotta on the back. "Great play! Now let's get a run, Cyclones, and win this thing."

Laurie wasn't optimistic. Angela, Maggie, and Carlotta—the bottom of the batting order—were due up. Not one of them had managed to get the ball out of the infield all day. Maybe now her father would be sorry that she wasn't in the batting order.

Mrs. C started some noise and Laurie half-heartedly joined in. The cheering was a little forced after Angela grounded out. It died altogether when Maggie followed with an easy grounder to third. But it roared back louder than ever when the Belair player on third base threw the wet ball away. Maggie chugged into second with only one out.

Laurie felt dishonest standing and cheering with her teammates as Carlotta came to bat. She wanted the Cyclones to win, but part of her wanted to see Carlotta fail. She wondered how her father felt now. A bunt wouldn't do much good in this situation, and if Carlotta didn't bunt, Laurie was sure she would strike out.

Carlotta did bunt. The player on third charged, but perhaps remembering the bad throw she had just made, she chose to let the ball roll, hoping it would go foul. As the Cyclones screamed, it trickled down the base line. Howard waved his arms frantically, urging Maggie to run and the ball to stay fair.

The ball stopped in fair territory. Carlotta had a base hit, and the Cyclones had the winning run on third base. Laurie was excited now. She forgot the cold and rain and cheered her loudest for Li, who was stepping into the batter's box.

Li had a single and a walk already, and Laurie was confident that she would come through again. Li was patient. She worked the count to three balls and two strikes. The Belair pitcher whipped a fast ball, and Li swung. The ball shot off the bat with a satisfying crack that brought the Cyclones to their feet. Then they realized that it was hit right at the Belair shortstop.

The shortstop fielded the ball smoothly and threw to second for the force-out. All the player on second had to do was throw to first for the double play that would end the inning. She never got the chance.

Running as if her life depended on it, Carlotta slid into second, upending the helpless Bobcat before she could get off her throw. Maggie scored, and the Cyclones had won their opener.

Laurie jumped up and down and cheered with the others. She heard Grandma tooting the Jeep's horn in celebration. Mrs. C screeched over and over, "That's the way to play ball!"

It was great to be on the winning team, but Laurie wished

she had contributed to the victory. And with Carlotta in the batting order and hogging all the balls, when was she going to get her chance?

Victory Party

At their victory party at the Slice of Life pizza parlor, the players toasted each other with hot chocolate. Her teammates' spirits were high, but sitting around in a wet uniform was not Laurie's idea of a party.

"That's another thing about basketball," she complained to Howard, "as soon as the game's over, you take a nice hot shower."

Howard just kept repeating, "What a finish!" over and over again. It annoyed Laurie that he didn't seem the least bit concerned about her feelings.

Li squeezed into their side of the booth, pressing Howard up against the wall.

"Great game, Laurie!" she bubbled.

"Not for me it wasn't," Laurie mumbled.

"Come on," Li insisted. "You've only been playing for a month and you're in the starting lineup. How bad can things be?"

"Starting lineup," Laurie sulked. "I stand in the outfield watching you guys have all the fun on defense. Then I sit on the bench watching you bat. Whoopee!"

"I watched the whole game from the sidelines and I thought it was great!" Howard said.

"At least you're where you can keep up with my dad's strategy. When you're standing in the outfield, you might as well be sitting in the bleachers," Laurie complained.

Coach Preston led Carlotta over to their table, one arm draped over her shoulders. "We showed them our best today!" he enthused.

Laurie's temper flared. "Some of us didn't even get a chance to catch a ball," she snapped.

She climbed over Li and headed for the door.

"Laurie, where are you going?" Li called out.

"I'm going home," Laurie said. She would rather walk home in the rain than pretend that she was happy about the way she was being treated.

Just before stepping out into the rain, Laurie turned and shouted, "I want a chance to show my best, too!" She caught a glimpse of her dad's and friends' stunned faces before the door slammed shut.

Chapter 5

Slap in the Face

As she slogged home, Laurie's anger faded and started to turn into shame. How could she act like such a baby? The Cyclones had won, and a team victory was much more important than one player's performance. Her dad had taught her that, and she'd just shown him how not to be a team player.

When Laurie walked into the house, her grandmother greeted her with a warm smile. "Have a good victory party?" she asked. She looked behind Laurie at the door, expecting to see Coach Preston come in from the rain.

"Dad's still at the Slice of Life, Grandma. I walked home," Laurie said dully, kicking off her soggy sneakers.

Grandma raised her eyebrows. She looked as though she wanted to ask Laurie more questions.

"Well," she said instead, "why don't you go get into some dry clothes, and we'll talk about it later."

Laurie trudged up the stairs to her room. She peeled off her wet uniform and pulled on sweatpants and a T-shirt, then flopped onto her bed. She was exhausted. As she drifted off to sleep, she tried to stop thinking about her embarrassing behavior. But she also couldn't help wondering when she'd get the chance to contribute to the team.

Laurie's chance came sooner than expected. While she was eating breakfast the next morning, the telephone rang.

"I'll get it," she called. She scooted across the kitchen and picked up the receiver.

"Hello?"

"Laurie? It's Emily."

Laurie was surprised. She hadn't known Emily before softball season, and they had barely exchanged a word since. Why would she be calling?

"Hi, Emily. What's up?"

"I wanted to tell your dad that I sprained my ankle running up the steps to my house last night. The doctor says I can't play for the rest of the week."

Laurie's heart began to pound. This was her chance to crack the batting order.

"I'll get my dad," she said.

When Coach Preston got off the phone, he looked serious. "Well, Laurie, you're in the batting order for Friday's game. We'll work on your hitting after practice."

"That's great!" Laurie couldn't contain her enthusiasm, even though she knew it was wrong to feel happy about a teammate's injury. Then she remembered how terribly she'd behaved after the game, and her face fell. She hadn't talked to her dad since leaving him speechless at the Slice of Life.

She drew in a deep breath. Time to face the music. "Dad, I'm sorry for the way I acted yesterday. The team is the most important thing, and I was just mad because I couldn't—"

"It's okay, Laurie," Coach Preston stopped her. "Let's just move on and get you ready to play." Then he grinned and tugged her ponytail.

She grinned back, relieved.

Laurie couldn't wait to work on her hitting. She was restless in school. Then practice seemed to last forever. At last Coach Preston let the other girls go, and it was time for Laurie to show her stuff.

Coach Preston started her off with some lobs right over the heart of the plate. She lined the ball sharply and soon had Li, Howard, and Carlotta chasing balls all over the field.

Gradually, he started throwing pitches a little off the plate. Laurie kept right on swinging. She still made contact, but not with the sweet spot on the bat.

"Wait for a strike," he called.

Laurie kept hacking until the pitches were too wild to reach. Coach Preston called time.

"Take your normal stance," he told Laurie, "and find the outside edge of the plate with your bat. Anything wider than that, you've got to let go."

Laurie went through the motions, though her face burned at being corrected, especially in front of Carlotta. What did her father want from her? She'd been pounding the ball.

"And remember, the strike zone is from your knees to your armpits. Don't go after the high ones. All you can do with them is pop up."

Laurie forced herself to let a few pitches go by, but she was convinced she could have hit them. At last her dad seemed satisfied and threw strikes. Laurie hit them hard and finished on a high.

Now it was Carlotta's turn, and Laurie took her place at

shortstop. Carlotta swung only at perfect pitches, just as Coach Preston wanted, but she did nothing with them. Soon Li and Howard joined Laurie in the infield so they could more easily field the various dinks that came off Carlotta's bat.

Laurie used her mitt to hide the satisfied smirk that kept creeping onto her face. On Friday, everyone would get to see her and Carlotta hit. Then they would know who should be in the batting order and who should be watching from the bench when Emily returned.

But her father's words took away her satisfaction in an instant.

"Carlotta, can you come to the gym at lunch time tomorrow? I've asked Coach Landro to work with you. I think slap hitting might be a useful technique for you to learn."

"Sure, Coach, I'll be there," Carlotta said eagerly.

Laurie's jaw dropped. Coach Landro was the varsity coach. If her father felt anyone needed an expert to help with hitting, shouldn't it be his own daughter? Instead, he was helping Carlotta push her out of the batting order.

Laurie fumed quietly all the way home. She barely acknowledged Li, Howard, and Carlotta when her dad dropped them off. And she certainly didn't talk to her father. The second he shut off the engine, she shot into the house and up to her room.

Strategy

Laurie knew it was time for dinner, but she was still too angry to face her dad. She'd rather hole up in the family's computer room and work on homework than eat with someone who cared more about a near-stranger than his own flesh and blood.

"Laurie, may I join you?" Grandma stood in the doorway. When Laurie nodded, Grandma sat by her at the computer. "I know you're upset with your father, but tell him how you feel. He must have a good reason for what he's doing."

"He favors Carlotta over me," Laurie insisted. "Everyone is so impressed because her father is a pro."

"Is that what you really think? Come down to dinner and talk it over," Grandma coaxed gently.

"Are you sure Dad's having dinner? He might have to spend the time thinking up more ways to help Carlotta," Laurie snapped.

Grandma frowned. "Are you mad at me or your father, Laurie?" Her voice wasn't so gentle now.

Laurie hung her head. She shouldn't have snapped at Grandma. It wasn't her fault that Laurie felt cheated.

"I'm sorry, Grandma," she mumbled.

Grandma's face softened. "Come on," she said, patting Laurie's hand.

She followed her grandmother to the dinner table. Coach Preston looked up expectantly as Laurie came into the room.

"Dad, I want to learn to slap hit, too," Laurie demanded.

Coach Preston sighed, "Do you know what slap hitting is?"

"It's a way to keep me out of the batting order," Laurie answered.

"It's a way to take advantage of a player's speed," Coach Preston explained, "even though the player can't hit."

"Are you saying that I'm not a fast runner?" Laurie stood with her hands on her hips.

"Of course not, Laurie. You don't need to slap hit because when you make contact, you hammer the ball. You've seen Carlotta. Her best whack barely gets the ball out of the infield."

"So how does this slap hitting work?"

"What happens when Carlotta comes up to bat?" Coach Preston asked.

"The defense creeps in closer and closer because she tries to bunt every time," Laurie said.

"Right. Slap hitters square around as if they're going to bunt. But if the infielders charge, they slap the ball into the ground as hard as they can. They try to slap the ball between fielders or bounce it over their heads."

"So why don't you want me to do it?"

"What do you enjoy about hitting, Laurie?"

Laurie stopped and thought. She imagined the ball jumping off her bat and shooting up the gap in left center. "I like ripping a long one," she admitted.

"Slap hitters never get that feeling. They're up there to get on base the only way they can."

Laurie felt a little better. She knew her father had to make the best team he could with the players available. Laurie knew slap hitting wasn't for her. But if Carlotta could help the Cyclones score runs by learning to slap hit, he had to help her do it. But why did it have to be at his own daughter's expense?

Opportunity

Friday's weather was as beautiful as Monday's had been ugly. The combination of a great day and a chance to hit had Laurie racing for the field the moment she'd put on her uniform. The Newton Longhorns would be the opponent for this second straight home game.

Laurie forced Howard to show her the lineup before she started warming up. As expected, she was batting ninth. But the surprise was that Carlotta had moved up to sixth, ahead of Angela and Maggie. Carlotta had been working on slap hitting for just three days. Was it making that big of a difference?

Jesse would be the starting pitcher for the Cyclones. League rules limited a pitcher to ten innings a week, and Dawn had used seven of hers on Monday. Because Jesse didn't have Dawn's speed or power, she needed lots of help from the defense. Laurie expected some action in center field today.

When the first batter of the game lofted a high fly ball in her direction, Laurie handled it with ease and thought, "This is going to be my day."

The Cyclones wasted no time in pummeling the Longhorns' starting pitcher. Jackie hit a long home run to put them ahead 3 to 0. Later in the inning, Carlotta bunted past the pitcher's mound for a base hit. Laurie came to the plate with the bases loaded and two outs.

Grandma and Mrs. C were in the stands again, and Laurie heard Mrs. C scream, "Come on, Laurie!" This time Laurie welcomed the attention. She planned to hit the ball deep and put the game away. This was her opportunity to earn a permanent slot in the batting order.

The first pitch was a fastball, right at eye level. Laurie took a mighty cut—and missed.

"Hit a strike, Laurie," her father called.

Laurie stepped out of the batter's box and took a practice swing. She thought of the nice, easy strokes she'd been taking in practice. Then she was ready.

The pitch came in knee high, but as Laurie swung, it dipped into the dirt. She missed again. Blood pounded in Laurie's temples. This was her big chance, and she had two strikes already. She was so shaken that she forgot to step out of the box.

Before she was ready, the next pitch was on the way. Laurie swung wildly and the inning was over. Stunned, she stood at the plate as the Longhorns ran off the field. Li came up behind her and handed her a mitt.

"You'll get them next time, Laurie," she said.

Luckily, none of the Longhorns hit the ball to center that inning, because Laurie couldn't get her at bat out of her mind. She'd done everything just the opposite of the way she'd planned. Maybe she didn't belong in the batting order.

In the third inning, Laurie got to see Carlotta slap hit for the first time. Carlotta squared as if to bunt, and the infielders charged. Carlotta pounded the ball into the hard dirt in front of home plate. The ball took one big hop over the player on third and out into left field for a single.

Laurie's turn came with Carlotta on second and two outs. This time she waited until the count was two balls and no strikes. When the pitcher came in with a fastball, Laurie stroked it. The ball sailed on a high arc into left field. Even though it was caught for an out, Laurie felt better. At least she had looked like a hitter.

It seemed as if the Cyclones would win easily...until the last inning. Then, with two outs, one of the Longhorns singled to right. The next batter smacked a line drive that landed in front of Angela in left field.

When the following hitter walked to load the bases, Coach Preston called time and came out to the mound. Laurie could see Dawn staring at her father as he talked to Jesse. She knew Dawn wanted to come in and pitch.

Coach Preston left Jesse on the mound, probably because the batter was a slim left-hander whom Jesse had already struck out twice. This time, though, the player hit a hard line drive to right field. Maggie took one step in, then realized the ball would carry over her head. By the time she ran the ball down, the batter had circled the bases for a grand slam. The stunned Cyclones were losing, 4 to 3. The sudden turn of events had silenced even Mrs. C.

The next batter grounded out to Li, and the Cyclones came in for their last licks, needing a run to tie the score.

Jackie lifted their spirits when she started the inning by slamming a double down the left field line. Then Jesse hit a long fly ball to center that was caught, but Jackie tagged up and ran to third after the catch. That left Carlotta with a chance to knock in the tying run with only one out.

The infielders crept in closer until their coach signaled them to stop. Laurie peeked at her father. He gave the take sign. Carlotta squared around but let the pitch go by for ball one. The infielders hadn't charged, afraid that Carlotta would slap the ball past them.

Laurie's eyes were glued on her dad. He touched his belt, then he rubbed his face with his hands.

Li gasped. "It's a suicide squeeze."

Laurie shook her head in confusion. "What's that?"

"Jackie's going to run on the pitch, and Carlotta's going to bunt. Unless Jackie gets tagged out at home, we'll tie the score."

Mrs. C led the fans in screaming Carlotta's name. The pitcher pumped her arm and whipped the ball toward home. Carlotta squared. Jackie raced for home as the pitch crossed the plate.

Carlotta let the pitch go by.

The Longhorn catcher caught the ball cleanly and jumped out from behind the plate. Jackie skidded to a stop and tried to run back to third. As she spun around, the cleats on her left foot stuck in the ground. Her knee twisted and she fell, her face white with pain. The catcher flipped the ball to her teammate at third base, who reached down and tagged out a writhing Jackie.

Coach Preston yelled for time and ran to his fallen player. He knelt over her for a moment, then yelled for someone to call 911. Eileen's father ran on the field, his cell phone to his ear.

Carlotta stood near home plate, her head hanging. Dawn knelt at Jackie's side and comforted her friend.

Li grabbed Laurie's arm, and the two of them went to get Carlotta. When Laurie touched Carlotta's shoulder, the stunned girl turned and fell into Laurie's arms, bursting into tears.

"I was concentrating so hard on the pitcher, I forgot the sign meant I had to bunt," Carlotta sobbed. "The pitch came in too high, so I let it go. I didn't know it was a suicide squeeze."

Laurie felt tears well in her own eyes. She had been so jealous of Carlotta that she almost felt responsible something bad had happened. Li steered them both over to the Cyclones' bench.

At last a wailing siren signaled the ambulance's arrival. A paramedic examined Jackie's knee and supervised as she was loaded onto a stretcher. Grandma Preston offered to ride in the ambulance with Jackie, since the girl's parents hadn't been able to make it to the game.

Coach Preston came over to Carlotta. "You made an honest mistake," he said as they watched the ambulance pull away. "I don't want you to bat when you're so upset. I'll use a pinch hitter."

Laurie had forgotten that the game wasn't over. Tears rolled down Carlotta's cheeks as Coach Preston told Wheezy to grab a bat. Everyone was so distracted that they sat in stunned silence as Wheezy popped up to the infield for the out that ended the game.

Disabled List

As Howard crammed equipment into the back of the Jeep, Laurie and Li tried to get Carlotta to leave the bench.

"Your dad will want to go to the hospital, Laurie. I can't do that. Jackie will be so mad at me!" She started to sob again.

Laurie felt a tap on her back. Mrs. C was poking her with her cane.

"Carlotta can come with me," she said. "I don't dare go near the hospital. The way I walk, the doctors will lock me up."

Carlotta didn't smile at Mrs. C's kidding, but she did stop crying.

"But how will you get home, Mrs. C?" Laurie asked.

"We could hitchhike," the old woman joked, "but I don't want to teach Carlotta bad habits. Mr. Riley is going to give us both a ride."

Li hugged Carlotta. "I'll call you tonight. Try not to feel bad."

"Injuries are part of sports," Mrs. C said, putting an arm around Carlotta. "One time I beaned one of my own teammates with a throw. Knocked her out cold in front of ten thousand people. Accidents happen to everyone."

Judging from her hanging head and slumped shoulders, Laurie didn't think Carlotta looked reassured, but she let Mrs. C lead her to the Rileys' car.

Coach Preston drove to the Compton Central Hospital emergency room. Laurie, Li, and Howard stared out the windshield, each lost in thought.

At last Li broke the silence. "I remember when I sprained my ankle in the state basketball tournament. One minute you're happy and excited, part of the team. The next you're wondering if you'll ever play again."

"I feel bad for Carlotta," Laurie said. "She made so many great plays in our first two games. All she'll remember now is her one mistake."

"It's my fault," Coach Preston sighed. "I should have called time and made sure she knew what I wanted her to do."

Howard was too depressed to enter the day's stats in his laptop. "What if Jackie's out for the season?" he wondered.

"What will the Cyclones do without a catcher or a cleanup hitter?"

The Cyclones played the tough Bingham Bears next. Their star pitcher, Tawana Johnson, was rumored to be unhittable. Laurie had played against the talented player during the basketball season. If Tawana pitched half as well as she sunk three-pointers, the Cyclones were in trouble. Her stomach flipped as she thought about batting against Tawana.

When the group entered the emergency room, they spotted Grandma Preston sitting with Jackie's father. Coach Preston went over to talk while Laurie, Li, and Howard found seats on the other side of the room.

Soon Grandma joined them. "How is she?" Laurie asked.

"Nothing is broken," Grandma answered, bringing smiles to their faces. "It's a strained knee. Jackie will be as good as new in no time."

Laurie squeezed Li's hand. She wanted to find a phone and tell Carlotta the good news. But just then, she saw Coach Preston shake hands with Mr. Morgan and walk toward them.

"How long before she can play again?" Howard asked, pushing his glasses back into place.

"Jackie will be on crutches for a week or two. Then we'll see," he answered, running his fingers through his hair. "But she's done catching for the season. Her father and I don't want her putting stress on her knee."

"Who's going to be our catcher?" Li asked.

"Beats me," he shrugged. "If only Mrs. C were about seventy years younger."

Hot Rod's Take

Laurie called Carlotta as soon as she got home. Carlotta was relieved that the injury wasn't serious. And when she heard that Jackie would be back playing soon, at least as the designated hitter, she was downright cheerful.

"Mrs. C really helped me," Carlotta said. "She was a professional and she made lots of mistakes. She says that I'll probably never miss another sign after what happened today."

"That reminds me. We're planting Mrs. C's garden in the morning," Laurie said.

"I can't make it this week, remember?" Carlotta said. "My dad's home opener is tomorrow. I'll be at the stadium."

"Right. Cheer loud for me."

"I will. See you!"

Laurie smiled as she hung up the phone. She was glad Carlotta was feeling better. But shouldn't she be a little worried about who was going to catch for the Cyclones? Laurie wondered how she'd feel if she had caused an injury and hurt the team's chances to win. She doubted she'd feel very cheerful, no matter what anyone said to cheer her up.

The next morning Mrs. C was waiting in the back yard when they arrived. Howard used his laptop to diagram where she wanted the tomatoes, corn, zucchini, and beans planted. Then they got to work. To their surprise, Mrs. C painstakingly lowered herself to the ground and began planting a border of marigolds around the edge of the garden.

"Are you sure you're up to that, Mrs. C?" Howard worried.

"If I can't get back up, you can bury me right here," she joked. "The ground's nice and soft. Now, let's get back to work."

Laurie enjoyed having something to keep her hands busy while she tried to think of what the Cyclones could do to salvage their season.

"Who's going to be our catcher?" Laurie asked.

"Emily's the obvious choice," Howard said, "but she has such bad hands that teams would run wild against her."

"No way Wheezy is up to it," Li offered. "A catcher has to have a lot of stamina."

They spent the morning talking about ways to shuffle the lineup without coming up with a plan they thought would work. When Coach Preston brought lunch, Laurie didn't waste any time asking him for his ideas.

"Well," he said as he helped Mrs. C into her lawn chair, "I know who to ask for advice. Mrs. C, you know our roster. Is there anyone you think would make a good catcher?"

"I thought you'd never ask," beamed the old woman. "A catcher needs to be physically fit, have good hands, a strong throwing arm, and be a tough competitor. Sound like anyone you know?"

Laurie suddenly realized that everyone was staring at her.

Chapter 6

On the Job Training

"You've got to be kidding," Laurie said.

"Think about it, Laurie," Coach Preston urged. "You'd be involved in every pitch. No more standing in the outfield waiting for something to happen."

"Remember how you said Carlotta and I got to have all the fun?" Li coaxed.

"And you hated being left out of the strategy sessions on the mound," Howard reminded her.

Laurie grew excited. She pictured herself whipping the ball around the infield, yelling to keep the fielders alert. If softball had a point guard, the position she loved to play in basketball, the catcher would be it.

"I'll give it a try," she said, steadily meeting her father's eyes.

Howard and Li high-fived. Mrs. C clapped Coach Preston on the back with her cane hard enough to knock him off balance.

By the time the kids had eaten lunch, Coach Preston was back with two duffle bags full of equipment. He handed one bag to Laurie. She was amazed at how heavy it was. She dumped the contents on the grass.

"Everything you need to play the most demanding position on the diamond," said Mrs. C.

Laurie put on the shin guards. Each had two buckles connected to elastic straps. She picked up the chest protector and put her head through the top loop. Jackie was much bigger than Laurie, so the straps were too loose. She turned her back to her father, and he pulled in the slack.

"Now that it's adjusted, you won't need help putting it on," Mrs. C assured Laurie.

Laurie pulled the mask over her face and stuck her hand inside the catcher's mitt. She shuffled over to where her father was pacing off the distance from the pitcher's mound to home plate. Halfway there she got a fit of the giggles.

"I feel like a monster in one of those cheesy old horror movies you like to watch, Howard."

"You'll soon be glad you're armor-plated," Mrs. C said.

Laurie shuffled to her position. There she crouched and practiced catching her father's lobs. As she got used to the bulky catcher's mitt, he picked up the speed of his pitches.

Mrs. C kept an eagle eye on Laurie's performance.

"Shift your feet! Don't backhand the ball," she scolded when Laurie reached for an outside pitch. "As long as the ball stays in front of you, you're in control. Once it's behind you, the base runners go wild."

Laurie's stomach knotted. What if she messed up and cost the team a game?

"Let's see how you do with a batter up there," Mrs. C snapped. "Li, grab a bat. Howard, it's not that I don't trust you, but I've seen you play pepper. You be the fielder."

The first few times Li swung, Laurie flinched and closed her eyes. If Li missed, the ball bounced off Laurie's mitt or chest protector.

"You won't get hit by the bat as long as you stay back where you belong," Mrs. C promised. "Don't reach for the ball. Let it come to you."

As the afternoon wore on, Laurie started to feel more comfortable. The first time she caught a ball cleanly after Li swung and missed, everyone applauded. Laurie just wished she had more than two days to practice before the Cyclones played the Bears.

On Sunday afternoon, the group, including Carlotta, met in Mrs. C's back yard. Mrs. C was snoozing in her lawn chair when they arrived. Carlotta's excited chatter woke her up.

"My dad went two for four and robbed a guy of a base hit. The whole stadium was cheering," Carlotta said.

While Carlotta raced to her left and backhanded an imaginary grounder, Laurie said softly to Mrs. C, "Jackie called Carlotta this morning. She said there are no hard feelings and that she'll be on the bench to root for us while she's hurt."

"Leave it to a catcher to know how to be a good teammate," Mrs. C answered. "Now let's do some work so the Cyclones can earn some cheers this week."

Under Mrs. C's watchful eye, Laurie, Li, and Carlotta loosened up their arms while Coach Preston and Howard paced off the distance from home to second base. Today Laurie was going to practice throwing out base runners.

This time Howard pitched while Coach Preston acted as the batter, swinging and missing on every pitch. Carlotta and Li took turns being the base runner and covering second to catch Laurie's throw.

Li broke from first as the ball crossed the plate. Laurie

fielded the pitch and jumped up throwing. She spotted Carlotta and whipped the ball toward her. It sailed wide of the base.

"Don't watch Carlotta," Mrs. C shouted. "Throw to the base. The base doesn't move."

The advice helped. Laurie started putting most of her throws right on the bag. But she was taking so long that Li and Carlotta would have been safe every time.

"You're winding up too much," Mrs. C told her. "You can get away with that in the outfield. But not behind the plate. Bring your arm back to your ear and snap that throw to second," she encouraged.

By the time they were ready for a break, Laurie was pleased. Li and Carlotta hadn't slid into the base, but even if they had, Laurie thought she'd have thrown them out about half the time. She just hoped that her skills would be good enough in tomorrow's game.

Foul Up

As soon as the Cyclones' bus arrived in Bingham, Laurie got to work. She put her gear on quickly so she would have as much time as possible to get used to handling Dawn's pitches. Dawn's fastball twisted her mitt and bent back her fingers. But Laurie bet the loud smack of the ball flying into her mitt had the Bingham batters squirming. She was glad to be catching Dawn's pitches instead of swinging at them.

Then she remembered that Tawana Johnson was a dominating pitcher, too. Tawana was the tallest player in the league, as she had been in basketball. By the time she let go of a pitch, her body seemed to stretch halfway to home plate.

Laurie tried to concentrate on her catching duties. Coach Preston had suggested a simple set of signs. Laurie would put down one, two, or three fingers, but only as a decoy. Dawn would throw a fastball unless she shook her head. Then the pitch would be a changeup. Laurie would set up inside or outside, and Dawn would aim at the target.

While the Cyclones batted in the first, Laurie rested and drank lots of water. The heavy catcher's equipment made her sweat, and she didn't want to become dehydrated. With the mighty Tawana on the mound for the Bears, there was little chance she would come to bat this inning since she was ninth in the lineup.

As Laurie had predicted, the Cyclones went down in order. Ready or not, it was time for her to go behind the plate. As Dawn fired her fifth and final warm-up pitch, Laurie yelled, "Coming down!" She caught the fastball cleanly and fired a strike to Li at second base. Li flipped the ball to Carlotta, who whipped it to Eileen at first. Eileen threw across the diamond to Jesse. Jesse tossed it to Dawn, and the Cyclones were ready.

Laurie checked to make sure the outfielders were in position. Wheezy was playing in Laurie's old spot in center, but she wouldn't get to bat. Emily's ankle had healed, and she would be the designated hitter.

The leadoff batter stepped in, and Laurie got into her crouch. She felt crowded with the batter in front of her and the umpire leaning over her shoulder from behind. But with each pitch she grew a little more comfortable. The first inning was uneventful; Dawn retired the side on two grounders and a strikeout.

The game was still scoreless when Laurie came to bat in the third inning. Tawana's first pitch was an inside fastball. Laurie tried to jump out of the way, but the ball was on her before she could react. It hit her bat and bounced back to Tawana for an easy out that ended the inning.

Howard caught Dawn's warmups as Laurie scrambled to get her gear on without delaying the game. "At least no one else has gotten a hit against Tawana," she consoled herself.

When the first Bingham batter singled to left field, Laurie knew she was about to be challenged. The runner was almost certain to try to steal. Laurie went over Mrs. C's tips in her head: Stay back, snap the throw from your ear, and aim at the base.

On the first pitch, the runner broke. Laurie came up firing and threw the ball perfectly. There was only one problem. Li slipped and fell as she ran to cover second. The ball sailed into center field, and the runner ended up on third. Laurie knew she had made a good throw, but she couldn't tell if it would have been in time, if Li hadn't fallen.

The next batter hit a sharp ground ball to short. The runner broke for the plate, and Laurie jumped out to block it. Carlotta fielded the ball and threw home in one fluid motion. Laurie caught the ball and slapped the tag on the sliding runner an instant before the opponent's foot touched home plate. The umpire bellowed, "You're out!" His words were one of the best sounds Laurie had ever heard.

Dawn got out of the inning without allowing runs, and the

game stayed scoreless until the fifth. Laurie came to bat with two outs. She heard her dad call her name and looked down to the first base coaching box. Coach Preston touched the bill of his cap—the take sign.

"He doesn't trust me not to swing at a bad pitch," Laurie thought.

The first pitch came in at a frightening speed. It was ball one. Laurie peeked at Coach Preston, and the take was on again. The next pitch was high, and Laurie didn't even bother to look at her father. She knew she had to take.

Laurie took a strike, then checked with her dad. He motioned for her to hit away. Tawana threw the next two pitches in the dirt, and Laurie had a walk.

"Run at the crack of the bat," her father told her when she reached first. Li hit a little looper over the shortstop's head, and Laurie was off and running. The ball dropped in as she reached second, but she had to hold there because the shortstop gloved the ball on the first hop.

The Cyclones' bench was up and cheering. Emily came through with a ground single up the middle. Laurie raced for third. When she saw Howard windmilling his arm, she rounded the base and headed for the plate.

She took one peek and saw the rightfielder come up with the ball. Laurie sped across home plate just before the catcher could slap a tag on her. The Cyclones were ahead 1 to 0.

As soon as she could escape her excited teammates' hugs, Laurie chugged some water and started putting on her gear. She looked up in time to see Dawn hit a long fly to left.

The team rose as one to cheer wildly while Li and Emily sped around the bases. But the left fielder made a running catch, causing Dawn to kick the ground in frustration as she neared first base.

Laurie was afraid that the lost hit might make Dawn lose concentration. But she pitched just as steadily as before. The teams went to the seventh and final inning with the score still 1 to 0.

Laurie was tired, and her legs ached from squatting behind the plate, but she felt happy. The Cyclones were about to win a close game, and she had been involved in nearly every play.

Dawn would have to retire the Bears' three best hitters, the most dangerous being Tawana. The inning started with an easy groundout to Li. The next batter singled off Dawn's changeup, and then Tawana came to the plate.

Laurie called for an inside fastball. Tawana tried to check her swing and popped the ball straight in the air. Laurie tore off her mask and dropped it on the ground. She stood at the plate waving her arms, yelling, "Mine, mine!"

She seemed to have the ball lined up, but then she realized it would come down a little behind her. Laurie took a step back. Her foot landed on some object, and down she went. The ball landed next to her in foul territory.

Laurie looked to see what had made her fall. Her face burned with shame. She had tripped on her own mask. Tawana would get another chance.

"Shake it off, Laurie," she heard Coach Preston call. She snatched the mask, slipped it on, and quickly resumed her position behind the plate.

The count went to two balls and two strikes. Laurie set up for the inside fastball again. Tawana must have guessed what was coming. She took a half-step back, swung, and drilled the ball high and deep to left field. When it sailed over Angela's head, Laurie knew the game was over. She waited at home plate, but Angela's relay had just reached Carlotta when Tawana crossed the plate with the winning run.

All the exhaustion of the hard day hit Laurie at once. She dragged herself over to the bench where she sat, slowly taking off the heavy gear while the Bears congratulated their star player.

Li touched her arm. "You caught a nice game, Laurie. We'll win the next one."

Laurie could only stare blankly at her friend. Dawn sat down beside her.

"You're going to be a great catcher. Don't worry about that pop-up."

"I thought I was finally going to help the team," Laurie sighed. "Maybe I'd be better off in the outfield."

"Hey," Dawn said sternly. "She hit my best fastball. Sometimes you have to give the other team credit for beating you."

Dawn grabbed Laurie's elbow and steered her to the third base line where the Cyclones were shaking hands with their opponents. Laurie forced herself to look each of the Bears in the eye as she shook hands. She didn't want her sulking to take anything away from their victory. "But," she admitted to herself, "it's easier being on the winning side."

Tune Up

Li, Howard, and Carlotta tried to make Laurie feel better on the way back to Compton. That night, when Mrs. C phoned to learn the score, she took personal responsibility for the mistake.

"I'm the professional catcher, and I never taught you how to handle your mask," she insisted.

"What should I have done?" Laurie asked.

"You were right to pull your mask off right away, but you've got to hang on to it. Just before you catch the ball, throw it away. That way it will never be where it can trip you up."

"I wish I had thought of that," Laurie said.

"I know you," Mrs. C said firmly. "You'll never make that mistake again."

"Maybe not," Laurie thought, "but what other ones will I make? How much more is there that I don't know?"

The next day during lunch time, Jackie hobbled over to talk to Laurie. Laurie stiffened, waiting for Jackie to make fun of her.

"Welcome to the club," Jackie said.

"What club?" Laurie replied, her arms crossed in front of her chest.

"The trip-over-your-own-mask club," Jackie laughed. "I did the same thing my first year behind the plate."

"Did it cost the team a game?"

"No," Jackie admitted, "but I made lots of other dumb mistakes that did. It takes time to learn a new position."

Laurie was relieved. Maybe no one expected her to be a superstar catcher after all.

"How's the leg?" Laurie asked.

"Good enough for me to ride the bus Friday. I'll be at the game to give you my expert advice."

"I'll be listening for it," Laurie smiled.

Mercy

For Friday's game in Parkside, Jackie was on the bench to lead the cheering. Laurie noticed that she was carrying her crutches under her arm as often as she was using them to walk. It wouldn't be too much longer before the Cyclones would have her big bat back in the lineup.

Catching Jesse's pitches was another new experience for Laurie. While Dawn's fastballs had threatened to tear off her mitt, Jesse's deliveries settled in with a gentle plop. The problem was, if her pitches were easier to catch, they were also easier for batters to hit.

The Ponies, who had split their first two games, were using a slightly built left-hander as their pitcher. Laurie watched her warm up and felt her confidence rise. Compared to Tawana's, this pitcher's serves looked like batting practice.

The Cyclones hit the ball hard in their first at bat, but right at the Parkside fielders. Then it was the Ponies' turn to hit. Since Jesse was pitching, Dawn would play third base. She was tested with runners on second and third and two outs. Laurie gave Jesse an inside target. The batter smashed the ball on one hop right at Dawn. It bounced between her legs, and two runs scored.

Carlotta beat out a bunt for the Cyclones' first hit. She tried to steal second and appeared to have made it. But the umpire called her out for leaving first base too soon. Angela followed with a double, but died on second.

In the fourth inning, Laurie's inexperience showed. With runners on second and third, the Parkside player bunted down the first base line. Laurie's instinct was to field the ball. She chased it down, then realized no one was covering home plate. She froze as the batter reached first and a run scored. When the next batter hit a long double, the rout was on.

Parkside loaded the bases in the fifth, and Coach Preston brought Dawn in to pitch. During warmups, Laurie noticed that her pitches lacked their usual pop. Sure enough, the first batter singled to make the score 7 to 0. The next batter walked to load the bases. When the Ponies' cleanup hitter lined one up the alley in right center, all three runners scored.

Maggie got the ball to Li, and Laurie stood at the plate screaming for Li to throw the ball home. Instead Li held the ball and ran off the field. Laurie gaped as the rest of the Cyclones trotted in to the bench. Her father crossed the diamond and shook hands with the Parkside coach. What was going on?

"Mercy rule," Howard explained when she finally could shake her disbelief and make her way to the bench. "If a team is ten or more runs ahead in the fifth inning, that's the game."

Laurie didn't know whether to feel disgusted that the Cyclones had been humiliated or glad she wouldn't have to bat again. Her dad had made her take a strike each time up, but once she was on her own, Laurie had swung at everything that was thrown. She had struck out twice.

Laurie gritted her teeth, congratulated the Ponies, and shuffled to the bus. She'd take her catcher gear off on board. The sooner they left Parkside, the better.

Chapter 7

R and R

Laurie had thought that her father might call a Saturday practice because the Cyclones had played so badly. But he seemed to sense that what the team needed more than anything was a couple of days to forget about softball. Their next game wasn't until Tuesday, and Monday's practice would be time enough to face their problems.

On Saturday Laurie, Li, and Carlotta worked at Mrs. C's. Howard was attending a baseball card show but had promised to bring them pizza at lunch time.

The girls pulled weeds and watered the delicate green sprouts under Mrs. C's watchful eye. Laurie was proud Mrs. C seemed to come to life when they were around. During their first visit, she had spent most of the time sleeping. Now she was interested in her visitors and eager to talk with them. The friends found they enjoyed talking with her, too.

"What can we do to get better, Mrs. C?" Carlotta asked. "It seems the harder we try, the worse we get."

"That game yesterday was embarrassing," Li added.

"When I played for Rockford, we were under a lot of pressure to win," Mrs. C sighed. "The owner kept telling us we had to win to draw fans. If people didn't show up, we'd drop out of the league."

"What happened?" Laurie asked.

"We tried so hard, we stunk," Mrs. C snorted. "We got blasted two games in a row at home. The stadium was half-empty, and we thought we were through."

"But the team didn't fold," Carlotta pointed out. "We saw the clippings. You played for four years."

"Our manager took us aside before the third game. He told us we were young, healthy, and playing ball. What more could we ask? Why didn't we just enjoy it for as long as it lasted?"

The friends looked at one other. Laurie thought of the fun she'd had with practice, pepper, and pickle. Why shouldn't the games be just as much fun?

"Did you come back and win the title that year?" Carlotta asked.

"No, we were never that good," Mrs. C chuckled. "But we won our share of games the rest of the way, and had a heck of a good time. That's what you girls should do."

"Let's start with a pizza party," came Howard's voice from behind them.

Laurie turned and saw her dad and Howard coming across the lawn. Coach Preston was carrying two pizzas while Howard had his laptop and enough baseball cards to open his own shop.

"Why are you so happy?" Laurie teased. "Did you get a Yogurt Berra card or something?"

"That's Yogi Berra," Howard smiled. "These are the brand-new Hudson Valley Renegade cards. Wait till you see Carlotta's dad."

Carlotta squealed as Howard handed her the card. Lorenzo Sanchez was sliding headfirst into third base. Howard gave

Carlotta the rest of the set. In exchange, she promised to have her father sign some cards for Howard.

Regrouping

Coach Preston agreed with Mrs. C that the players were trying too hard. Everyone was worried about making a mistake. He promised to come up with a plan for helping the Cyclones relax.

The weather cooperated. Monday's practice was held under a cloudless sky, with a cool breeze to keep the sun's warmth in check.

The whole team's spirits lifted to see Jackie walking without crutches. The doctor had given her permission to take batting practice. Just the sight of Jackie taking her cuts cheered everyone up.

Carlotta was especially bubbly, and when Coach Preston talked to the team, Laurie found out why.

"We've got a big week ahead, starting with a home game tomorrow against Millbrook. If we relax and have a good time, I know we can get back on the winning track."

Laurie thought her father was up to something. He looked as if he was fighting to hold back a grin.

"There is a schedule change for the Belair game. We'll be playing at eleven o'clock Saturday morning instead of Friday after school. The bus will leave here at eight-thirty."

The players started murmuring to one another. Why would they play on Saturday? And why was the bus leaving so early? It was only a fifteen-minute bus ride from Compton to Belair.

"Carlotta," Coach Preston offered, "maybe you can explain the rest."

Carlotta popped up, her eyes shining. "My dad has arranged for us to play our game against the Bobcats in Dutchess Stadium before the Renegades' game. We'll get to visit the clubhouse and be special guests at the Renegades' game against Lowell."

The Cyclones let out the biggest cheer Laurie had heard all season. She couldn't wait to play in a real stadium with a scoreboard and outfield fences. Now she'd get to experience a little of the excitement Mrs. C had known in her days as a player.

Howard stood speechless. Laurie knew he would start planning how to get the most autographs possible, as soon as he got over the shock.

Then Laurie remembered. They had promised Mrs. C they'd work in her garden on Saturday.

"Dad, what about Mrs. C?" Laurie asked. She saw Li's face fall as she remembered their commitment.

"Who do you think is going to chaperone?" Coach Preston grinned.

Perfection

Mrs. C was behind the bench for Tuesday's game against the Millbrook Tigers. Grandma Preston sat beside her. Laurie looked at the crowded bleachers and the rows of lawn chairs behind the backstop. It was the best turnout of the year. She knew the fans were there as much to enjoy the beautiful weather as to see the ball game, but their presence still pumped her up.

Dawn threw for about five minutes, hitting the target every time. She grinned at Laurie and said, "I'm ready. Let's save the rest for the game."

Laurie was on the bench watching the Tigers take infield when her dad sat beside her.

"You know how we talked about taking it easy and not worrying about mistakes?" he asked.

Laurie nodded.

"Well, that goes for me, too. I've been trying to control things too much. Today when you bat, you're on your own. Swing at the pitches you think you can hit."

Laurie grinned. "Thanks, Dad. I won't let you down."

Dawn blew away the Tigers in the first two innings. Then the Cyclones hit some hard shots, but right at the Tigers' fielders. In the third inning, Carlotta bunted a ball toward first. The first baseman charged in to field it and reached to tag her. Carlotta slid headfirst into the base and was safe.

One out later, Laurie came to the plate. She peeked at her father, but only to see if Carlotta was stealing. It felt good to know that he trusted her enough to let her succeed or fail on her own.

The first pitch came. Laurie started to swing, then checked when she realized it was high. The next pitch was way inside, and Laurie just managed to duck out of the way in time. Now she looked for a fastball. The pitcher would have to throw her a strike.

The pitcher rocked and fired. Laurie started her swing and turned her hips into the ball. The ball struck the sweet spot on the bat so perfectly, it felt weightless. Laurie raced for first as the ball sailed on a line into the gap in left center field. Carlotta scored all the way from first, and Laurie coasted into second with a double.

She heard Mrs. C's unmistakable howl. "Way to rock 'em, Laurie!"

Li was called out on a pitch that Laurie thought was outside. Li didn't argue; Coach Preston didn't allow his players to complain to the umpire. But Li's tolerance didn't stop Mrs. C from yelling, "Give me a break!" at the top of her lungs.

Emily hit a ground ball to short. As Laurie raced for third, she skipped over the ball. The distraction was enough to make the Tiger shortstop lose concentration, and the ball got by her.

Howard waved his arm frantically. Laurie rounded third and headed for the plate. She kept her eyes on the Tiger catcher. When Laurie saw the catcher stretch toward the pitcher's mound for the throw, she slid behind home plate. The catcher reached for her but missed the tag. As Laurie skidded past home, she reached out and slapped the plate with her left hand.

Mrs. C's was the first voice to yell, "Safe!" but the umpire backed up her call. Laurie brushed herself off and accepted her teammates' congratulations.

The score stayed at 2 to 0 as the innings rolled by. Laurie was amazed at how smoothly Dawn worked. Nearly every pitch was a strike, each with so much steam that the Tigers were helpless.

When Laurie joined her teammates on the bench for the last of the sixth, she realized that the players and the fans had grown silent. She turned around and saw that even Mrs. C was quiet, watching the game with none of her usual saucy comments. Ordinarily if the Cyclones were ahead, everyone would be smiling and joking. What had happened to their new relaxed attitude?

Laurie turned to Li. "What's going on?" she asked.

"It's bad luck to say," Li answered tightly. "Go check the score book."

Laurie hurried to the end of the bench where Howard had left the book. She studied it for a moment without noticing anything unusual. She couldn't resist looking at her own stats: two for two with a run scored and a run batted in.

Then she glanced at the Millbrook side of the book. Her throat closed a bit. The Tigers had not had a single base runner. Laurie had been so involved in getting out each batter that she hadn't realized Dawn hadn't given up a hit or a walk. Nor had the Cyclones made an error. Dawn was pitching a perfect game!

Laurie looked for Dawn. Jackie had an arm draped over her shoulder and was whispering in her ear, but Laurie couldn't tell if Dawn was listening. She stared straight ahead, occasionally massaging her pitching arm.

Laurie chugged some water and took her place in the on-deck circle. She was almost relieved when Maggie hit a fly ball to the center fielder for the last out. It would have been hard to concentrate on hitting when thoughts of the final inning had her head spinning.

Dawn stared in from the mound. Laurie knew the fastball was Dawn's best pitch, and she didn't plan on calling for anything else this inning. If the Tigers were going to break up the perfect game, they would have to hit Dawn's best.

When the first batter struck out, waving at a high fastball, the fans erupted. Mrs. C screamed, "Two more, baby!" Laurie whipped a bullet to Jesse at third. In seconds the Compton infielders had thrown the ball around the horn and back to Dawn.

The next batter swung at the first pitch. She hit it off the handle, a twisting pop fly over Jesse's head and into short left field. The crowd groaned, expecting the ball to drop in safely. Carlotta, running at full speed, bent and plucked the ball out of the air, an instant before it could hit the ground. Laurie roared until her throat burned. Two outs.

Fittingly, the Tigers' best hitter was up. She was the only hitter in the lineup whom Dawn had failed to strike out.

The player took a strike, Dawn's fastball zooming into Laurie's mitt. She swung and missed at the next pitch, a fastball low and away. One strike to go.

Laurie set her target just off the plate. The steely nerved Tiger wasn't tempted. Ball one. Dawn threw her best fastball, a high riser, and the batter fouled it back to stay alive. Laurie set up inside, and Dawn backed the player off the plate with ball two.

Laurie set the target low and away again. Dawn's arm whipped back, then forward. The pitch rocketed toward home plate. The batter swung and tipped the ball. Laurie's mitt shot up and grabbed it. She wheeled, waved the ball in the umpire's face, and was rewarded with a bellowing "STRIKE THREE!"

Laurie raced for the mound and embraced Dawn. In seconds they were knocked down and buried under a pile of celebrating Cyclones. Laurie heard later that Grandma had to grab Mrs. C to keep her from hobbling out and throwing herself on top of the heap.

Postgame

The excitement of the perfect game kept Laurie bubbling. She sat between Li and Howard at the large round table in the Slice of Life, as the team devoured a "Pig Out" sundae. The sweet creation filled a huge pasta bowl, but it was no match for the jubilant Cyclones.

When the last spoonful of chocolate sauce had disappeared from the bottom of the bowl, Coach Preston stood up.

"Ladies, great game today. Super pitching, Dawn, and a great job behind the plate, Laurie."

Laurie flushed with pride. At last she could look back at a game without regretting mistakes or lost opportunities.

"And fine work by our defense," he went on, resting a hand on Carlotta's shoulder. "A perfect game is a team accomplishment."

The Cyclones cheered, banging their spoons on the side of the big bowl.

"We have five games left. Jackie will be back in the lineup on Saturday, and I don't see any reason why we can't make this a great season."

Laurie grinned. She had a feeling the excitement had only just begun.

Chapter 8

Take Me Out to the Ball Game

On Saturday, Laurie could tell from the high spirits on the bus that the Cyclones were ready to play. Grandma and Mrs. C shared the front seat, and every few minutes a burst of their raucous laughter would drown out the noise the whole team made.

Howard was firing questions at Carlotta about Dutchess Stadium.

"You'll see for yourself in a few minutes," she laughed when she couldn't keep up with his demands for information.

In addition to his laptop, Howard brought along an album filled with Renegade cards. His shirt pocket bulged with the special felt-tip markers he used to collect autographs. A digital camera hung around his neck.

"Don't forget to unload your celebrity gear before you coach third base," Laurie teased.

"Don't worry," he replied seriously. "I wouldn't risk damaging any of these babies."

Laurie chuckled and leaned back in her seat. Gazing down from the Newburgh/Beacon Bridge, she saw sailboats cutting back and forth, framed by the rolling green hills that flanked the Hudson River. A flotilla made from a half-dozen huge, flat-bottomed barges was guided through the shipping channel by a tiny tugboat. It was a beautiful day, and Laurie knew it was only going to get better.

Ten minutes later, the bus pulled into the stadium parking lot. The Bobcats hadn't arrived yet, so the lot was nearly empty. Laurie recognized the Sanchez family's blue car pulling up alongside the bus. Lorenzo Sanchez climbed out, a broad grin on his face. Carlotta's younger sister scrambled out after him. Martina Sanchez emerged from the passenger side door, then leaned back inside to take out the baby in the car seat.

Carlotta scrambled to the front of the bus, and Coach Preston let her be the first person through the door. She ran to her father and wrapped her arms around him. As the others stepped down, Carlotta introduced her parents and sisters.

When it was Howard's turn, Mr. Sanchez said, "Howard, we meet at last. I've alerted all my teammates. They're ready to sign anything and everything for you."

Howard was tongue-tied, but nodded his thanks. He snapped a close-up of the family with his camera.

Mr. Sanchez led the team to the locker room, where he gave the official greeting.

"Welcome on behalf of the Hudson Valley Renegades. We're happy to share our beautiful stadium with you today. You and the Bobcats will use our locker room. We'll dress with the visiting team. I'm sure many of you have been to major league games in New York City, but has anyone ever been in a clubhouse before?"

The girls shook their heads. Laurie spotted Mrs. C, who was just hobbling in with Grandma.

"Mrs. C has," she called. "She played in the All-American Girls Professional Baseball League."

"Our setup wasn't this fancy though," Mrs. C laughed.

"It's a pleasure to meet a fellow pro," Mr. Sanchez said as he shook Mrs. C's hand. "Now I've got to go meet the Belair team."

Coach Preston and Howard went to check out the field and learn the local ground rules. Mrs. Sanchez took Carlotta's sisters, Grandma, and Mrs. C to their box seats.

The players dressed as quickly as possible. Laurie couldn't wait to set foot on a professional field, and she was sure her teammates felt the same way because everyone was scrambling to be the first out the locker room door. Everyone, Laurie noticed out of the corner of her eye as she strode toward the door, except Emily. Laurie was puzzled until she remembered that Jackie was now the designated hitter. That meant that Emily would be on the bench. Laurie remembered how tough it was for her, a rookie, not to be included in the lineup. It must be especially hard for a veteran player to lose her spot

Laurie slowed, then headed to where Emily sat listlessly knotting a shoelace.

"Don't feel bad, Emily," she comforted. "The way things change on this team, you could be back in the lineup before sundown."

Emily forced a smile. "Thanks, Laurie, but this team doesn't need me. I know I'm not the greatest on the field." She drew in a deep breath. "I'm glad Jackie's back. I didn't like being the DH anyway. It's no fun watching the game except when it's my turn to hit. I've just been waiting for her to get healthy so I could quit."

Laurie was floored. "Are you sure you—" she began to ask.

"Yeah, I'm sure," Emily cut in. "I'm going to try my swing

with a different sport. The golf course will be opening up soon, and I'm signed up for lessons."

"Does my dad know?"

Emily nodded. "He understands. This is my last game, so let's go win it." She stood, ready to hit the field.

Laurie didn't know what to say, but she followed her teammate out the door. Emily knew what was best for her, but Laurie couldn't help feeling bad. She couldn't even imagine leaving the team now.

As soon as everyone was ready, Carlotta led them through a concrete tunnel and up a flight of steps to the dugout. Laurie felt like a real ball player as she peered up at the lush, green grass, the neatly raked infield, and the giant scoreboard in center.

Coach Preston jumped up from the bench, his fungo bat in his hands. "Let's take it, ladies," he yelled and led the team onto the field.

A few parents had joined Grandma, Mrs. C, and the Sanchez family, but since it was still an hour before game time, the stands were largely empty. Mrs. C's "Cyclones rule!" echoed through the stadium.

But by game time, a modest crowd had arrived. Parents and friends of players on both teams were there. Some of the Renegades' fans had come early to enjoy the spring sunshine and an extra ball game.

Li led off the game with a walk. She was on second base with two outs when Jackie came up to bat for the first time since her injury. On the very first pitch, she let everyone know she was back. Jackie stepped into a fast one and launched the ball on a line deep to left field. The Belair fielder broke back at the crack of the bat, but she had no chance. The ball soared over her head and rolled all the way to the fence, 325 feet from home plate. When Jackie scored, the whole Cyclone team streamed from the dugout to greet her. Laurie thought Carlotta looked the happiest of all.

When it was Belair's turn to bat, Laurie squatted behind the plate and looked over the Cyclone defense. Angela, Wheezy, and Maggie seemed dwarfed by the huge outfield they'd have to cover. She hoped Jesse would be able to hold the Bobcats in check.

Jesse pitched her usual game. She threw strikes and relied on her defense. The Bobcats scored four runs against her, but key plays by the Cyclones kept the score close.

With two runners on in the third, Li ranged down the right field line to catch a twisting pop fly and end a rally. In the sixth inning, Carlotta made the play of the game. A Bobcat batter hit a ground ball between short and third. Carlotta knocked it down, but had no play at first base. She faked the throw to first, wheeled, and picked off a base runner rounding third.

The Cyclones came up for their last turn at bat trailing by a single run, 4 to 3. Carlotta led off. She had bunted twice earlier, so the infielders charged toward the plate the instant she squared around. Carlotta slapped the ball into the hard dirt in front of home plate. The ball took a kangaroo hop over the head of the first baseman and dribbled down the right field line.

Carlotta was off like a deer, her long strides eating up the base line. Laurie thought she would stop at second, but Carlotta wanted more. She sped past the bag, through Howard's stop sign, and headed for third.

The right fielder scooped up the ball and fired a strike to third base. Carlotta slid in a cloud of dust. Her foot met the fielder's glove, and the ball squirted loose. She was on third base with no one out.

By now many of the Renegades' regular fans had arrived, and they howled their approval of Carlotta's speed and daring. They had barely quieted down when Angela lined a single up the middle to tie the score.

Maggie was next. Coach Preston had his hands on his belt. Laurie thought about what he had said during the first week of practice: Teams that can move runners up with a bunt win games. She crouched in the on-deck circle and hoped that Maggie could lay one down now.

Maggie bunted toward third. The player on third charged and thought of throwing to second. But Angela had gotten a great jump, and the Bobcats had to settle for the out at first. Laurie would have a chance to knock in the winning run.

Laurie tried to shut off all the noise in the stadium. She settled into the batter's box and focused on the pitcher. The first pitch was high and fast, just the type Laurie might have swung at a month ago. This time she let it go by for ball one.

Angela leaned toward third as the pitcher rocked again. This one was waist high, on the outside corner of the plate. Laurie went with the pitch, smashing it in between first and second. As she raced for first she could see the right fielder charging. Would Angela try to score?

Laurie rounded first as the fielder came up throwing. She

spun around and watched the ball and Angela race for the plate. It was no contest. Angela sped across the base and into the flailing arms of her teammates. The Cyclones were ahead.

Coach Preston wasn't taking any chances. He brought Dawn in to pitch the last inning while Jesse slid over to third base. After Jesse's soft tosses, Dawn's ball seemed supersonic. Three Bobcats in a row went down swinging as the noise from the stands got louder and louder.

The Cyclones were on a roll.

First Ball

The teammates showered and changed into jeans and T-shirts in record time. Laurie suggested that they all wear their uniform caps. The girls made their way to their box seats along the third base line while the Renegades were taking infield. The crowd greeted them with a fine round of applause.

Howard was in his glory. He typed data into his laptop with one hand. The other held a foot-long hot dog buried in mustard and relish. Grandma Preston had stored his cards safely in her tote bag. Mrs. C was waving a Renegades pennant.

When practice was over, the crowd stood for the national anthem. Laurie watched the flag wave in the gentle breeze, the players in their crisp, white uniforms against the green grass.

Mrs. C ended the anthem by shouting, "Play ball!" at the top of her lungs. Then instead of squatting behind the plate, the Renegades' catcher trotted over to the stands in front of the Cyclones' seats.

The announcer's voice boomed across the ballpark. "We have a special guest in the stadium this afternoon. Sally 'Hot Rod' Carnovski, three-time all-star in the All-American Girls Professional Baseball League, will honor us by throwing out the first pitch."

The Cyclones cheered until they were hoarse. Mrs. C took the ball from the catcher. He backed a few feet away and waited. The "Hot Rod" snapped a throw from her ear that landed in his mitt with a satisfying smack. Laurie noticed Mrs. C had tears in her eyes as she waved to the crowd.

Mrs. C turned to face the Cyclones. "Which one of you set this up?" she squawked.

The girls shook their heads. Howard shrugged his shoulders.

"It was my dad," Carlotta admitted. "I've been talking about you nonstop ever since I found out you were a professional player. He's grateful I have you to look up to."

Mrs. C wrapped her arms around Carlotta. "Tell him he's made an old lady feel pretty special."

The game was a thriller. The Renegades jumped out to an early lead, then held on for dear life. Lowell threatened to rally in the seventh, but Lorenzo Sanchez cut down the tying run with a great relay throw to home plate. The crowd leaped up to cheer.

Mrs. C whooped with joy. "Your dad is heading for the big time!" she told Carlotta, who beamed with pride.

The crowd remained standing for the seventh inning stretch. The Renegades' mascot burst out of the Renegades' dugout carrying a cordless microphone. He trotted over to the Cyclones' box seats and held the mike in front of Mrs. C. The announcer asked Hot Rod to lead the crowd in singing "Take Me Out to the Ball Game." Mrs. C waved the microphone away.

"I was a catcher," she yelled. "The only thing I've got left is a catcher's voice. I don't need a mike."

The Cyclones, their parents, and friends followed Mrs. C's lead and sang for all they were worth.

"Is there anything better than being part of a team?" Li asked Laurie when the shouting died down.

Laurie smiled brightly. She couldn't predict how the Cyclones would do for the rest of the season, but she knew that now they really were a team.

Chapter 9

Playing for Pride

Team spirit was soaring. If the Cyclones could stay hot, they had a chance to catch the league leading Bingham Bears. If Bingham lost just one more game, they would fall into a tie with the Cyclones. Then the final game of the season at Compton would decide the championship.

The Cyclones did stay hot. Dawn shut out the Longhorns 4 to 0. They got their revenge on Parkside 3 to 2 in front of a noisy crowd at Compton. Then they battered the Tigers 11 to 1, this time the mercy rule working in the Cyclones' favor.

Laurie found that she was not even tempted to swing at bad pitches anymore. She knew now that her father and Mrs. C were right. If she were patient, she would get better pitches to hit.

The game had slowed down for Laurie. Early in the season, it had seemed like she had a split second to decide whether to swing. She had to commit herself before she knew if the pitch would be in the strike zone. Now she could tell in plenty of time if she should check her swing.

She talked about her progress with Mrs. C at the Slice of Life as the team celebrated its rout of the Tigers.

"I'm not surprised your batting's improved. You've developed the catcher's eye," Mrs. C told her. "Handling so many pitches gets you used to the speed. Can't you tell when the ball leaves Dawn's hand where it's going?"

"I guess I can," Laurie admitted.

"It's the same thing at bat. You know what to look for now."

Laurie gave Mrs. C a hug before leaving to join Carlotta, Li, and Howard in their booth. Li and Carlotta were chatting and giggling, waving their arms to emphasize their points. But Howard sat staring at his laptop, a dazed look on his face.

"What's wrong with you?" Laurie asked. Li and Carlotta stopped and noticed Howard's strange behavior.

"Check out my e-mail from my friend in Bingham," Howard said, turning his laptop toward Laurie.

She looked at the display and read aloud, "'Final score: Parkside 7, Bingham 6.'"

Laurie looked up from the screen. Howard lifted his gaze, and Laurie saw that his eyes burned with excitement. Suddenly he shot up from his seat, sending two sodas and a half-eaten slice of pizza sailing off the table.

"We're still alive!" he shouted.

Laurie, Li, and Carlotta jumped up and ran from table to table, spreading the news.

"Dad, we can win the championship!" Laurie screamed in Coach Preston's ear.

When the news reached Dawn and Jackie, who were seated on the far side of the room, the eighth-grade stars stared at each other. Jackie banged her empty soda can on the table to get everyone's attention, and Dawn stood up.

"The final game of the softball season will be played here in Compton tomorrow afternoon," she said. "The Cyclones host the Bingham Bears. The winner is the league champion."

"It's the last game Dawn and I will play for Compton Middle School," Jackie added, standing beside her friend. "We don't plan on losing."

"Come out and support the Cyclones," Dawn urged, "and we'll show Bingham that we're the best in the league!"

Howard jumped to his feet and whooped, waving his arms over his head. Everyone stood and cheered for the Cyclones.

"Now all we have to do is back up our bragging," Laurie thought.

Collision Course

Most of the student body joined the usual crowd of parents and friends who turned out to watch the Cyclones' games. The big crowd and the chance to match her skills against the league's best had Laurie feeling sky-high. She'd learned a lot since the first time she faced Tawana Johnson. Standing in against the big right-hander had made her queasy during their first matchup. Now she welcomed the challenge. Laurie knew that even if the Cyclones lost today, they would be champions in their own minds, no matter what the standings showed.

As expected, the game was a pitchers' duel. Dawn and Tawana were in control. In the fourth inning, the Bears' speedy center fielder beat out a slow roller.

"She'll be running," Mrs. C squawked, and Laurie knew she was right.

Laurie called for a fastball and gave Dawn an outside target.

"She's going!" Coach Preston yelled.

Laurie fielded the pitch cleanly and came up firing. Her throw ate up the distance between home and second, and seemed to slow the runner in her tracks. Li never had to move her glove as Laurie's throw exploded into the target. The sliding runner tagged herself out.

But the Cyclones were having no luck with Tawana's lethal serves. Singles by Li and Jackie in different innings were all the attack they could muster. Laurie felt she had taken some good swings, but she had struck out and grounded out in her two at bats.

In the top of the seventh, the Bears mounted a threat. Tawana led off with a line drive to right. Maggie was playing deep against the powerful hitter. She cut the ball off with a nice backhanded play, but Tawana slid safely into second with a double.

Coach Preston called time and went out to talk to Dawn. He waved his infielders over. Laurie pulled off her mask and joined the group surrounding the mound.

"They'll probably bunt. Field the ball and listen for my voice. I'll tell you where to throw it."

The infielders started to go back to their positions, their expressions serious. Coach Preston's voice stopped them.

"Ladies, if we don't win this game, Hot Rod is going to chew us all out. Now I know we can outrun her, but we'll never escape that voice. So let's get out of this jam!"

With laughter breaking the tension, the Cyclones hustled back to their positions.

The batter did bunt, right in front of the plate. Laurie scrambled out and grabbed the ball. Her father's voice rang out,

"First! First!" so she flipped the ball to Eileen. Tawana advanced to third. A fly ball could break the tie.

The next batter went after Dawn's first pitch, an inside fastball. She hit the ball off the handle, and it headed for shallow left field. Laurie heard the Bingham coach yell, "Tag up!" and she knew Tawana would be coming.

Carlotta backpedaled. Angela charged. Carlotta called and made the catch. She threw the ball toward home, but with her momentum carrying her away from the plate, the ball covered the distance slowly.

Laurie could feel the ground vibrate as Tawana thundered toward her. Why did it have to be the biggest player in the league trying to score? Carlotta's throw was on line, but it seemed to take forever to reach her.

Laurie jumped in front of the plate, her left leg in the base line. She braced herself as the ball and Tawana arrived at the same instant. Laurie slapped the tag on Tawana, pressing the ball into the mitt with her bare hand. Tawana jabbed her shoulder into Laurie to try and knock the ball loose. The collision launched Laurie backward, and she hit the ground with a thud. Her chest protector was twisted around her body. One shin guard hung by a single strap. But she held the ball high in her bare hand for the umpire to see.

"You're out!" And the crowd roared.

Dawn helped Laurie to her feet and steered her toward the bench. Laurie gasped for breath, still clinging to the ball. Finally, she let Li take it from her hand and throw it back to the umpire.

Facing the Ace

Coach Preston sat next to Laurie on the bench.

"Are you sure you're all right?" he worried.

"I'm fine, Dad," Laurie assured him. She was due up fourth this inning, and there was no way she'd let her father take her out of the game.

"Then let's get a run," he said with a grin and trotted out to first.

Angela and Maggie were easy outs. If Carlotta made an out, the game would go to extra innings. Laurie knelt in the on-deck circle, still wearing her shin guards. She was exhausted, and her body was starting to ache in too many places to count. If only the game could end right now.

Carlotta squared and slapped at the ball. Tawana charged off the mound. She was as accomplished a fielder as she was a pitcher and hitter. The ball hit home plate and bounced high in the air. Tawana paced under the ball as Carlotta sped down the base line.

The second the ball was within reach, Tawana grabbed it in her bare hand, wheeled, and fired. "Safe!" shouted the umpire. Carlotta had beaten the play by an eyelash.

Laurie's mouth became dry as she bent to unhook her shin guards. She forced herself to take deep breaths as she took a practice swing. It was all up to her now. She knew in her heart that she could hit Tawana's pitches. This was her chance, maybe the last chance this season, to prove herself.

Laurie choked up on the bat and stared at Tawana. The pitch sped toward her. She swung and fouled it straight back into the backstop for strike one.

Tawana fired again. Laurie was a split second late, but she got the fat part of the bat on the ball. She lined it down the right field line. She was halfway to first, when the ball curved foul. She had come so close. Now she was in a hole with two strikes.

Laurie took her time getting back into the batter's box. She thought Tawana would try to trick her now and get her to swing at a bad pitch. The ball came in high, and Laurie let it go.

The catcher burst out from behind her, firing a throw to second. Laurie had been so focused on Tawana that she hadn't even seen her father give the steal sign. Carlotta slid as the throw sailed over the player on second and into center field. Carlotta popped up and made it to third where Howard leaped up and down, pumping his fists.

Laurie dug in. She shut out the noise of the crowd and stared at Tawana's right hand, which gripped the ball. A belt-high fastball rocketed toward the plate. Laurie swung and heard a satisfying crack. The ball soared past Tawana's outstretched glove, over the player on second, and into the outfield.

Laurie raced down the base line to first. She jumped on the bag with both feet, turned to be sure Carlotta had scored, then let her father embrace her. As the Bears filed solemnly off the field, the Cyclones and their fans charged onto it.

Carlotta joined Laurie and Li in a group hug. Howard nearly hurt himself from jumping and leaping around so much. Only Dawn and Jackie mixed tears with their celebrating. The Cyclones had won the championship, but they had played their last game for Compton Middle School.

Happy Recap

The Slice of Life overflowed with celebrating players and fans joining the normal Friday night rush. Laurie's body ached from the collision with Tawana, but she didn't care. The season that had begun in frustration had ended in triumph. The Cyclones had won the championship just as Howard had predicted. But Laurie knew that even Howard could never have imagined the twists and turns the season had taken.

Coach Preston stood to speak, but as soon as the players at one table would quiet down to listen, another group would erupt in cheers and laughter. He was about to give up when a piercing whistle cut through the din and silenced the room.

"That's another trick I learned as a catcher," Mrs. C said with one of her rasping laughs. "Now give the coach your attention, or I'll do it again."

Everyone laughed, then focused on Coach Preston.

"I'm proud of all of you for not giving up on yourselves or the team," he said, turning to meet the eyes of each of his players. "That's why we're champions today."

There was another round of cheering, but when Mrs. C placed her fingers near her mouth, the cheers quickly died.

"Our new players made great contributions and worked hard to get their skills up to speed," he continued, smiling at Carlotta, Li, and Laurie, who beamed with pride.

"And our veterans provided the leadership we needed when things were going badly. Dawn, you never gave in to a batter. Jackie, you helped the team even when you were hurt and couldn't play. I know you'll both be successful players in high school. None of us will ever forget you."

Dawn and Jackie stood to the longest cheer of the night, their arms wrapped around each other, their tears mixing with laughter. They let go of each other long enough to wave their teammates to their feet for one final tribute.

Over the next hour, the pizza parlor gradually emptied as the players and their parents left for home. Soon Laurie, Howard, Li, and Carlotta were the only Cyclones left.

As the friends got ready to leave, Howard asked, "What are you guys doing this summer?"

"I'll be at basketball camp the first week of vacation," Laurie said. "I've never gone to a summer camp before. I'm really excited."

"I'm trying a new sport," Carlotta offered. "Soccer. There's a summer rec program starting in a couple of weeks."

"Cool!" Howard grinned. "Is it just for girls?

"Boys and girls. You guys should join."

"Count me in," said Li, kicking an imaginary soccer ball with her instep.

"Me, too. I love soccer," added Howard, trying to imitate Li's moves and stumbling. "Haven't you guys ever noticed my fancy footwork?" he joked after he recovered.

"You're with us, too, Laurie, when you get back?" Carlotta asked.

Laurie thought about spending the summer with her friends after she returned from camp. There was no question. She wanted to be in on the fun.

"Well?" Howard asked.

Laurie looked at her friends' eager faces and giggled.

"Of course! And think, you didn't even have to twist my arm this time."

The four friends laughed together.